PRAISE F
JEROME CHARYN

"His books constitute the highest kind of literary art... absolutely unique among American writers."

—*Los Angeles Times*

"A contemporary American Balzac....Jerome Charyn has been re-creating the absurdity, the frenzy, and the menace of contemporary life, using wit and imagination and style."

—*New York Newsday*

"His sentences make a mournful and sensational clatter, like a bundle of butcher knives dropped on a cathedral floor....He grows monstrous cabals out of seeds sown and lays the groundwork for sagas to come. It's always bigger than you think."

—*Washington Post Book World*

"Charyn's imagery is stunning and his vision of the future is chilling."

—*Chicago Tribune*

"He has made [New York City] his universe and has turned it into something entirely his own. Atmosphere and language are all to Charyn....Charyn has peopled this novel with the quick and the dead, the crooked and the straight, the cops and the robbers, the innocent and the mendacious. Almost no one is what he or she seems to be....Only the mayor is a known quantity, and he, too, offers more than his share of the unexpected."

—*Washington Post*

"Jerome Charyn has long ranked among the most talented, intelligent, and persevering of my contemporaries; and his fiction has established a solidly developed body of achievement."

—Richard Kostelanetz

BOOKS BY JEROME CHARYN

HURRICANE LADY
THE BLACK SWAN
CAPTAIN KIDD
CITIZEN SIDEL
DEATH OF A TANGO KING
THE DARK LADY FROM BELORUSSE
EL BRONX
LITTLE ANGEL STREET
MONTEZUMA'S MAN
BACK TO BATAAN
MARIA'S GIRLS
ELSINORE
THE GOOD POLICEMAN
MOVIELAND
PARADISE MAN
METROPOLIS
WAR CRIES OVER AVENUE C
PINOCCHIO'S NOSE
PANNA MARIA
DARLIN' BILL
THE CATFISH MAN
THE SEVENTH BABE
SECRET ISAAC
THE FRANKLIN SCARE
THE EDUCATION OF PATRICK SILVER
MARILYN THE WILD
BLUE EYES
THE TAR BABY
EISENHOWER, MY EISENHOWER
AMERICAN SCRAPBOOK
GOING TO JERUSALEM
THE MAN WHO GREW YOUNGER
ON THE DARKENING GREEN
ONCE UPON A DROSHKY

EDITED BY JEROME CHARYN

THE NEW MYSTERY

Hurricane Lady

Jerome Charyn

Published by Warner Books

A Time Warner Company

The events and characters in this book are fictitious. Certain real locations and public figures are mentioned, but all other characters and events described in the book are totally imaginary.

Mysterious Press books are published by Warner Books, Inc.,
1271 Avenue of the Americas, New York, NY 10020.

Visit our Web site at www.twbookmark.com

Printed in the United States of America

First Printing: May 2001

10 9 8 7 6 5 4 3 2 1

Library of Congress Cataloging-in-Publication Data

Charyn, Jerome.
Hurricane lady / by Jerome Charyn.
p. cm.
ISBN: 0-446-67733-7
1. Television producers and directors—Fiction. 2. Models (Persons)—Fiction. 3. Coma—Patients—Fiction. 4. Rich people—Fiction. I. Title.

PS3553.H33 H87 2001
813'.54—dc21 00-040112

Mr. Lamplighter

1

He was coming out of Duck Soup with his *New York Times,* like a soldier of fortune stranded in L.A. He crossed Sunset, intending to have a tofu burger and carrot juice at his favorite health-food restaurant, The Source. He wandered into the lot where his little Dodge was parked. *Forbes* magazine had just named him the ninety-seventh richest man in America, but he always leased a Dart. All the residual money that fell into his lap from *Lamplighter,* his hit show, couldn't seem to change his habits. He still lived in a rented cottage near Muscle Beach, still bought his books at Vagabond and Duck Soup, still read his *Times* over a tofu burger. But he'd gone to the lot to get a handkerchief and a roll of quarters out of his glove compartment. It was almost noon. His Dart was broiling in the sun. His secretary must have sent him a fax while he was in Duck Soup. She was probably confirming his four o'clock appointment with a team of Italian producers. The fax paper curled obscenely onto the floor of the Dart; it couldn't have been a simple note from Natalie. She'd faxed him a document, something for him to sign. But he wasn't going to ruin his lunch.

As he reached into the glove compartment, a man must have crept behind him. It was ridiculous. Who the hell would rob you at high noon on Sunset Boulevard? He was almost angry. He wanted his tofu burger. But he didn't resist. He couldn't see the man's face. Was the guy wearing a mask? Was he a kid with a swastika engraved on his skull? Not one word was exchanged. Jocko felt a metal finger crawl up his forehead. Then his entire face exploded. And he was about to scream, *Natalie. I can't make my fucking four o'clock.* Even while the blood flew from his eyes, he was sane enough. I'm thirty-four, and I shouldn't have to die in a parking lot. And then Jocko was perfectly peaceful. Dying, he thought, was like learning how to swim . . .

He woke suddenly, brilliantly, with a great bell of light concentrated on a silver cross. Good, he thought, now I won't have to see the Italian producers. He knew where he was. Misericordia Hospital, north of Hollywood High. One of his cameramen, Sam Pick, had died of melanoma under a silver cross like that.

Jocko was hungry all of a sudden. A big fat nurse or sister of mercy fluttered past his bed. She had muscular calves, wore slippers with white stockings and a white institutional hat.

"Sister," he said, "I'd like a cheese omelet with a dry toasted bagel and a glass of grapefruit juice."

The nurse stopped in her tracks to stare at Jocko. "We don't have bagels."

"What about whole-wheat bread?"

"Shut up. You've been sleeping like a baby for six months. I had to diaper you, did you know that? You open your eyes, and the first thing you ask for is food. You don't say hello, or thanks, or how are you, or why am I here?"

"I don't understand. I was in a parking lot."

"Mr. Robinson," she said, "you were murdered, but you didn't stay dead. Now go back to sleep. And maybe, if you're a lucky boy, I'll bring you back a bagel in another six months."

He'd been in a coma, and nobody had bothered to knock on his door, discuss his bank accounts and *Lamplighter,* which had gone into its seventh year of syndication while Jocko was living on a diet of fortified muck piped into his belly. He was a little too weak to have long discussions on the phone, and the hospital refused to give him his own fax line. I'm a poor man, he muttered to himself. I'm a poor man. But it wasn't true. His fortune had multiplied during his six months of sleep. He was now the seventy-eighth richest man in America. His banker, Elliot Weinrib, had watched his money like a smart little devil, but Jocko was still very blue. If *Lamplighter* could increase its ratings without him (it was the number-one television show in the world), why the hell did he have to be alive? He'd created *Lamplighter*, nursed it through its initial slump, supervised each episode, and now it was moving like a bullet train, knocking out every other show in its slot. *Lamplighter* was the lord of Tuesday night.

Jocko grew more and more depressed. He called his production company, asked for Natalie, but Natalie was gone. He had a new secretary, Florence Trout, and she'd kept a detailed log of the faxes and calls he'd received. Jocko didn't care for her voice. It was too shrill. He had a terrible lust to fire her, but he didn't dare. He had to depend on someone he hadn't even met.

His nurse would shave him every morning and supply him with bagels from Farmers Market. She refused his tips.

"It's not a country club, Mr. Robinson. I bring you bagels for my own pleasure. You look pitiful in your hospital gown. I have to fatten you up."

He had nine or ten bagels a day, but nothing seemed to fatten him. Mostly he slept between meals. He didn't have the appetite to read or watch his own show. And once, rousing from a very wet dream in which he was making love to Florence Trout, the secretary whose voice he hated (she had a nightingale tattooed on her breast), he recognized the huge, jug-handled ears of Elliot Weinrib. His banker was sitting beside his bed, the first visitor the hospital had allowed him, and Jocko wasn't even notified.

"Elliot, did they catch the fucker who killed me?"

"I talked to the police. It was probably an addict who crawled out of the cracks. You're doing fine, Jocko. Rejoice. The bullet was lodged a couple of hairs from your brain. You were saved from oblivion by a tenth of an inch."

"Elliot, did the market jump over the moon? How did I get so rich lying in bed?"

"Stop feeling sorry for yourself. You were already rich, or can't you remember? And I won't even take any credit. Residuals keep pouring in."

"I want you to cancel the show. I'm sick of *Lamplighter.*"

"I don't have the power to cancel. And if I did, the network would break both my legs . . . and keep you here for the rest of your life. Don't knock *Lamplighter.* It's been kind to you."

And the son of a bitch walked out on Jocko, leaving him with all the fat, undecipherable pages of his stock-and-bond portfolio.

2

He had a curled scar where that crazy assassin's bullet had gone into his head, and it disfigured him, left Jocko with a bald patch that looked like a monk's tonsure or the mark of a pig's tail. He was only curious about one thing: Florence Trout, the secretary whom he'd never seen. He wouldn't talk to any of the honchos who were running *Lamplighter* while he slept under a silver cross. He got out of bed one morning, put on the clothes Elliot Weinrib had smuggled into Misericordia from Muscle Beach, and Jocko sneaked past the nurses' station, hailed a cab outside the hospital, drove to his production company in Santa Monica, and asked for Florence Trout.

His writer-producers hovered around him, showed him sketches and story lines for future episodes of *Lamplighter,* but Jocko wouldn't listen. "Where's Florence Trout?"

She arrived, looking like some pale sister of Sharon Stone, with a nervous tic near her mouth. The tic unsettled Jocko, almost made him ask if she wanted to move into Misericordia with him. But the hospital wouldn't have allowed Jocko a secretary. And he couldn't have survived with the shrillness of her voice.

Florence Trout stuck a sheaf of faxes in his face, held together with a golden pin. The pin fascinated Jocko, but he wouldn't read the faxes.

"Mr. Robinson, Mr. Robinson, what should I do?"

She chased him across the production office, and Jocko had to flee. He found another cab, went to Duck Soup, browsed through all the magazines, then had a tofu burger at The Source. Jocko was beginning to feel comfortable inside his own skin when he recalled the parking lot and the bullet that left him with a permanent pig's tail on his head. He ran home to Misericordia.

The hospital had become his hotel room, but no one dared kick him out. Jocko had pledged a million dollars to Misericordia. He was the hospital's little prince. His nurse continued to shave him and massage his legs, but she stopped bringing bagels from Farmers Market.

"You're healthier than I am, Mr. Robinson."

"I thought I was a murdered man."

"That game is over, sir."

But Jocko didn't suffer. He had whole-wheat bagels with bean sprouts delivered from The Source. His banker came to see him, Elliot Weinrib with the jug-handled ears, who had documents for Jocko to sign.

"Elliot, why are you plaguing me? I was in a coma, for God's sake. And you have power of attorney."

"Sign," Elliot said, removing a golden pin from one of the documents. Jocko smiled. It was the same sort of pin that Florence Trout had.

"You're banging her, aren't you?"

"What are you talking about?"

"Florence Trout. You had Natalie fired and stuck me with that bimbo."

"She's not a bimbo. She's an actress, a decent girl. And Natalie quit."

"Natalie was devoted to me," Jocko said.

"Natalie married a health-food fanatic. She's living in Big Sur. She had a baby. And you have to get out of bed."

"I'm not going back to *Lamplighter.* That's out of the question."

"It's your dad, Jocko. He's getting worse."

"Did he fall down? Is he in a coma? Did somebody shoot him in the head?"

"He rides up and down the elevator all day."

"That's his privilege. He has bodyguards, attendants around the clock. They can baby-sit with dad . . . in the elevator."

Elliot drove him to the airport. Jocko didn't have the proper clothes for Manhattan. It was January, and he was wearing casuals that would have served him well at Muscle Beach.

"Elliot," he whispered before he got to the gate. "If you want to bang Florence Trout, bang her on your own time. No more bimbos on my payroll."

He fell asleep on the plane, had most of the first-class cabin to himself, like some passenger on a spaceship. He bought a goose-down coat at Banana Republic after he landed at JFK. He bought winter loafers, wool pants, a vest that was perfect for the North Pole. He tossed his casuals in a trash can and waltzed out of Banana Republic in his new arctic clothes.

3

Jocko couldn't find his dad. Old Mr. Robinson wasn't in his penthouse on Washington Square. Jocko searched the elevators with Mr. Robinson's main bodyguard and nurse, Alfonso Walsh, a weight lifter who could have come off the sands of Muscle Beach. Jocko paid his salary. Mr. Robinson was only a minor millionaire. He didn't have residuals from all over the planet, like Jocko. He was a landlord who sank his bundle into one building, an elegant, decaying dinosaur.

Jocko had been born in the building, had grown up on the roof, had watched the Manhattan sun and moon until he went off to California and had hardly ever come back. Jocko didn't get along with his dad. Mr. Robinson had neglected his wife and only son, had kept a mistress in the same building. And Jocko had watched his mother waste away. She died during his junior year at college. Jocko had been saving his money, had planned to bring his mom out to California, to rent a cottage for her and him, but the nest egg he had was never enough. And he found himself in a killing mood whenever he thought of his dad.

Jocko wondered if the old man was mummified somewhere, had become encrusted inside a wall. He interrogated the bodyguard-nurse. "Alfonso, when did you see him last?"

"In the elevator . . . I got off to take a leak, and then he was gone."

The superintendent and the handyman scoured the basement and the back stairs. Neither of them could solve the mystery. Good, Jocko mumbled to himself. I won't have to bury him. And he wished the old man could permanently disappear like that. He went into his old bedroom to take a nap, looked out onto his own tiny terrace, rimmed with ice, and saw some shadow in a deck chair. His dad was out in the rain, and nobody had bothered to look.

Jocko grabbed his goose-down coat, opened the terrace window, and walked out to his dad, who was sitting in a San Diego Padres baseball cap and a simple shirt. Jocko wrapped his father in the goose-down coat. Mr. Robinson was whimpering and staring out into some windy void.

"What's the matter, dad?"

"I miss your mom."

And the old pain clutched at Jocko, the turmoil of his family life, and he couldn't be sure whom to love and whom to hate . . .

It was Jocko himself who'd become the baby-sitter. Alfonso could attend to other chores while "young Robinson" was around. Jocko would play pinochle with his dad. It was perfect as long as Jocko concentrated on the cards. But Mr. Robinson's mind would wander midway through a game and his mouth would fill with bile. "You're cheating, sonny boy."

"Dad, I've got nothing but a handful of jacks. You have all the kings."

"I'm not talking pinochle. You've been pulling money from my cash account."

"Dad, I was in a coma. I couldn't have gone into your accounts."

"Coma? Who's been keeping me in the dark? That charlatan of yours, that guy with the big ears?"

"He's been looking after you, dad. Elliot's your angel. He told me about the episode in the elevator."

"There was no episode," Mr. Robinson said, spitting into his handkerchief. "I like to ride up and down . . . I'm eighty years old. What else can I do? I've lost my appetite. I'd fall asleep if a bimbo undressed in front of my eyes. Who put you in a coma?"

"I'm not sure. I was shot in the head outside Duck Soup."

"Stop yakking like a Hollywood producer. What the hell is this Duck Soup?"

"A bookshop, dad, a meeting place for writers . . . it's where I get my *New York Times*."

"You blame me for your mother's death. You can't forgive your old man. And you've been sending Elliot Big Ears into my account."

"Give me a reason, dad."

"Spite. You could buy the San Diego Padres if you wanted, or the Chicago Bulls. And you want to make me feel poor."

Jocko pulled a checkbook out of his pocket. "What's missing, dad? I'll cover your losses right now."

"Playing Genghis Khan with your own dad. It's indecent . . . like pulling on your prong. I don't want your money. I want mine. Pick up your cards. I'll demolish you. And don't forget. It's ten dollars a point."

And Jocko fell right back into the flow of the game.

He lost nineteen thousand dollars to his dad in seven days, but he couldn't seem to fill the "hole"

in his dad's account. "It's peanuts," Mr. Robinson grumbled, "pinochle money." Jocko was still content. He'd stand out on his tiny terrace, smoke a cigarette, and wouldn't return to the pinochle table until the wind scattered the tobacco in his mouth.

But his little routine began to unravel. Elliot Big Ears must have given out his old telephone number to all kinds of people. It was the same number Jocko had had as a boy. His dad never disconnected the line. Mr. Robinson was waiting like a sickly spider for Jocko to repossess his room. And now the phone wouldn't stop ringing. Unemployed actresses, writers, technicians begged him for the tiniest gig on *Lamplighter. Lamplighter* was his baby, but he had nothing to do with the Leviathan that was spitting out show after show. He couldn't even fire his own secretary.

Miles Farmer called. Miles was another "hyphenate," a writer-producer like Jocko, but he'd never had any luck running his own show. They'd once worked on a television pilot together, about a gang of clever police dogs, but the pilot was never picked up. Jocko had brought him on to *Lamplighter* and had to let him go. Miles was an incompetent prick who'd managed to alienate the entire crew during his first week on *Lamplighter.* And Jocko felt remorseful ever since, as if he owed Miles a bit of his own blood.

Miles invited him to some party at a downtown club.

"I hate parties, Miles. You know that."

But he couldn't refuse. He was much too guilty.

He got off the phone, but his dad wasn't at the card table counting the money that Jocko owed him. Mr. Robinson was traveling again, up and down the elevator.

"I'll baby-sit him," Alfonso said. "It isn't a problem."

But it was Jocko who went out on the landing to baby-sit his dad. He rode up and down with Mr. Robinson, who welcomed voyagers in his car. The elevator had its own automatic controls, but Mr. Robinson would press all the buttons, chat with his tenants during the ride. He was lucid, cheerful, polite. And Jocko almost envied him, the landlord who piloted people into the partial sky of Washington Square.

4

Miles' party was at a place called the Elephant's Hide, a cabaret on Wooster Street. A beautiful girl sat on his lap the moment he arrived. She had a parrot tattooed on her shoulder. The parrot excited him, but not the girl, who had a sinister smile. She grazed Jocko with her hand, probed for an erection, but Jocko shoved the girl gently off his lap.

Miles appeared with a clutch of women producers. The women all wore neckties. They kept babbling about *Lamplighter,* called it a terrific show. They were handsome, lovely, with short hair, but they couldn't draw Jocko out of his own reclusive skin. One of the producers licked his ear, and Jocko heard a rumble inside his head, as if that same old assassin were visiting him again outside Duck Soup.

He screamed, apologized, had a vodka tonic at the bar. Miles kept pursuing him. "Jocko, help me out . . . the ladies will let me become a show runner if I can attach your name to the deal."

"Miles, is that why you invited me here . . . to parade me in front of your producer friends? Look at me. I was unconscious for six months. I can barely spell my own name."

"You're still Jocko Robinson, the greatest show runner in history. You don't have to spell."

There was so much enthusiasm in Miles' crooked face, so much need and desire, Jocko felt ashamed. He didn't belong at the Elephant's Hide, where women and men danced and kissed and made deals under a dark-blue light.

He tried to leave. Miles clutched his shoulder.

"Jocko, I'm begging you. Talk to me a little longer . . . the ladies will be impressed."

He put one arm around Miles Farmer, whispered in his ear. "If you ever call me again, I'll come out of my coma, Miles, and kill you myself."

He marched out of that dark, swaying platoon of bodies, which had warmed his bones, and went back into the chill of Wooster Street. It had begun to snow. Jocko felt like dancing, all alone, outside that fucking cabaret . . .

The snow never stopped.

He woke the next morning in his childhood bed with a white wall outside his window. He'd slept through the storm. The wind howled all night and Jocko hadn't heard a thing. Manhattan was blocked. There were twenty-two inches of snow, and Jocko had his own small mountain. Alfonso couldn't get in from Queens. The building had to survive with a skeleton crew. The schools were closed. The airports had shut down. The shops still had gates on their windows, and it was almost noon. "Manhattan's all mine," Jocko said like a mischievous boy, recollecting those earlier storms that had kept him out of school.

He heard someone whimper near the door. Mr. Robinson was standing in his robe. "I don't have any milk. Alfonso always brings me milk . . . and fresh bagels."

"Dad, look out your window. Nothing can move."

"I want my milk."

Jocko went downstairs into the storm. He had to wear the same galoshes he'd worn in high school. He trudged ten blocks in blinding snow, stumbled upon an all-night grocery, and bought the last carton of milk. He discovered three bagels at the bottom of a glass bin and claimed them for his dad. Jocko smiled at his conquests: a leaky carton and bagels that were as hard as bricks.

He plunged into the storm.

His dad's building had disappeared. The storm had claimed the building, swallowed it up, stuck it in some dimension where Jocko couldn't go. He was lost in Manhattan, without Duck Soup.

He bumped into a snow demon. The demon wore

a scarf that covered most of its face. Jocko was almost grateful. He'd follow the demon home to its snowy hell.

"Mr. Robinson, what's wrong with you?" the demon muttered under its mask.

It was Alfonso, who'd arrived from Queens. He led "young Robinson" around the corner, and the building reappeared.

Old Mr. Robinson was waiting at the door of the penthouse. He toasted the bagels and heated the milk. "Delicious," he said, after biting into one of those bricks.

Some of his glee began to come back. Jocko had the city to himself. The storm had crippled traffic. There wasn't a car moving out on the street. The snow had stopped falling, but the city's ploughs were trapped inside their barns, and no other vehicle could create a discernible path. There were only white hills, hills that reached above the storefronts. And Jocko sailed out into the street in his high-school galoshes. There was an incredible quiet, with only the slightest hum, as if snow could breathe.

Jocko didn't travel very far. A girl was caught in a snowdrift right outside his dad's building. She was buried under a mountain, with only her fists and her forehead in sight. Jocko unburied her with his own two hands. She could have been twelve. He wasn't sure. She was wearing gold-rimmed glasses, and the glasses, crusted with snow, made her blind. Jocko removed the glasses, wiped them with the mittens he'd borrowed from his dad. The girl had pale-green eyes that could have belonged to a beautiful insect.

"I was trapped," she said. "I couldn't breathe . . . but it was fun, like living in a soft submarine."

She couldn't have been twelve. Twelve-year-old girls didn't have such a precise vocabulary.

"I know who you are," she said, teasing Jocko. "Mr. Lamplighter."

"Who's been talking to you?"

"I haven't missed one episode," she said. "He kills me, Byron Little, and his tribe of bandits."

"I'm not Byron. I—"

"You walked away from your own show. But you're still Mr. Lamplighter."

She came riding off her white hill, and Jocko was startled, because she had a full chest under that girlish grin.

"What's your name?" he asked.

"Inertia."

She raced into the building and Jocko lost his balance and fell deep inside the snow.

5

He was excited and all upset. A new snow demon had entered his life. This "Inertia" was neither a woman nor a child. He couldn't seem to locate her in the building. The superintendent didn't know about any Inertias. And he couldn't find her again coming out of any snowdrift. Had he dreamt up the girl with the gold-rimmed glasses? Was he still in a coma?

She loved *Lamplighter,* and Jocko thought he might find a clue if he studied the show. He watched several reruns on Channel 12. It made him ill; looking at *Lamplighter* was like eating his own entrails. Byron Little was a disgraced prosecutor who stepped outside the law and "lit lamps" for the mob, brainstormed, discovered new tricks, choreographed incredible crimes, moved men and material about like a chess master, led criminals out of the dark. But the Lamplighter would also help the police solve heinous crimes, would use his raw intelligence, his own spectral vision to track serial killers and bank presidents who robbed the poor. His assistants were a tribe of jailbirds, prostitutes, drug addicts, computer pirates, whiskey priests who lent their own "legs" to Byron Little, their obsessive passions and expertise.

They were an insufferable group, a gang of crooks who behaved like little bishops and were holier than everybody around them. Jocko couldn't bear Byron's megalomania, his gang's smug relation to crime. And the *Lamplighters* he watched didn't offer Jocko a single clue about the girl in the gold-rimmed glasses.

Suddenly the man who'd slept for six solid months couldn't sleep at all. It was as if he'd crossed some bedeviled snowbank and landed on the other side of his coma. He'd pulled a childish woman out of the snow, chatted with her, listened to her ridiculous name, and couldn't seem to recover.

It was Alfonso who solved the mystery. He'd never seen Inertia, but there was a bunch of unsuccessful models living on the fourth floor. They were vagabonds who struggled to pay the rent. And it was Alfonso's guess that this particular phantom belonged to the bunch on the fourth floor.

Jocko knocked on the models' door. Someone peered out at him; it was the girl from that downtown cabaret, with the parrot tattooed on her shoulder.

"Inertia," he said. "I'm looking for Inertia."

She laughed. "Mr. Robinson, you can come inside and inspect the place, but we don't do tricks."

"I'm not the landlord." he said. "I'm just looking for Inertia."

"You'll have to speak to our manager, Mr. Miles."

"Miles Farmer?"

"That's him," she said, grinding her hips at Jocko and closing the door in his face.

He ran upstairs and called Miles, got his secretary on the line. "Mr. Farmer is out on the Coast, pitching to ABC."

"It's urgent," Jocko shouted. "Life and death."

"Mr. Farmer doesn't like to be disturbed when he's making a pitch . . . but I'll tell him that you called."

Jocko had the clout to locate Miles Farmer. He knew the president of ABC. He was Mr. Lamplighter, like Inertia said. But Miles might grow agitated if Jocko got in touch with ABC and tampered with his pitch.

Jocko ran to Wooster Street. He entered that cave, the Elephant's Hide, stood in the deep-blue light, saw other girls with a parrot on their shoulder dance in the dark, but none of them could dislodge his dream of Inertia.

His phone was ringing when he got back to Washington Square. He recognized Miles Farmer's shrill bark. "Help me, Jocko. I'm frozen. I can't make my pitch."

"Where are you hiding Inertia?"

There were all the familiar ogres at ABC, including the big boss, Perry Bowles. They were seven on their side of the table, scribbling memos among themselves, but they deferred to Bowles, a fat man in red suspenders who crippled the other networks in all the rating wars. Perry had the *nose;* he could sniff a potential hit, nurse it along, build it into a blockbuster. But he'd lost Jocko the last time, hadn't anticipated the ferocious charm of Byron Little, and he wasn't going to let another *Lamplighter* out of the room.

Miles sat on the far side of the table. He was trembling. The seven ogres never bothered to look at him. They were watching Perry Bowles, who seemed absorbed in the mark on Jocko's skull, that pig's tail.

"Jocko, do you really want to run a show again? I mean, the sound and the fury and all that."

Jocko bent toward Perry Bowles. "Tell the network not to worry. You'll always have Miles, even if I catch another bullet outside Duck Soup."

Jocko was jet lagged. He'd arrived in L.A. only an hour ago, had barely spoken to Miles. He didn't have a clue what Miles meant to pitch. And Miles couldn't open his mouth.

"Inertia," Jocko said, and all the ogres listened.

"The whole damn country has fallen into the muck. Where's devotion, where's sacrifice, where's love?"

One of the ogres chipped in. "Is it a cop show?"

"Robert," Bowles said, "you're interrupting the master, you're ruining his flow."

"I was thinking comedy," Jocko said. "With an inspirational beat. A bunch of models are living together. They all have a fatal flaw. Either they're a little too short, or much too tall. They move into a firetrap next to Washington Square, convert it into some kind of community center. They help abandoned husbands find their wives. They adopt drifters and runaways. They go after lawyers who steal the fortunes of old men."

Perry Bowles jumped up and down in his chair. "I get it . . . *Lamplighter* without the gore."

Miles couldn't move from the table. Jocko had to walk him out of ABC. Perry Bowles had green-lighted "*Lamplighter* without gore." Miles Farmer would have his new show.

"Now," Jocko said, "where are you hiding Inertia?"

"Inertia" was a nom de guerre, a mask the girls on the fourth floor liked to try on. They called themselves "Skeleton," "Sloth," "Lazybones," "Nightmare." They didn't have much of an occupation. They'd been dropped from the biggest agencies and had to model at very minor shows. Their preferred territory was the Elephant's Hide, where they drank, danced, and picked up men. It wasn't really prostitution, Miles explained. They were looking for sponsors, a champion who might bring them out of obscurity. Inertia's real name was Katinka Baer. Her father was a professional soldier stationed in Germany. Her mother was a nurse from Warsaw. Katinka had run off with a photographer at fourteen, had lived in Nice, Madrid, and New Orleans, had been on the runway in Paris and Milan, but she wasn't the right sort of gamin: her chest was too big. She was never the "bride" at a fashion show, never the darling of some couturier. She could prowl on a catwalk, draw the eyes of fashion photographers, but she didn't have the necessary sleek line. She was twenty-eight, and couturiers had stopped asking about Katinka Baer . . .

Jocko had gone to Miles' midtown office. The snow had disappeared from the ground, but sheets of ice fell from the glass towers, and entire avenues had to be closed. The ice dazzled Jocko, seemed like a splintered rainbow. But Miles couldn't produce Katinka Baer.

"You're her manager. Don't you know her schedule?"

He'd brought her roses, like some shy chevalier. He'd been nervous for a week.

"Jocko, they're headstrong girls. They do what they want. She promised to come. She gave me her word. Why would she duck a guy with a billion bucks?"

"It's simple, Miles. Money doesn't turn her on."

He walked home with the roses. There was a message from Elliot Weinrib on his machine. He called Santa Monica.

"Hey," Elliot said. "I have to find out from Perry Bowles that you were in L.A.?"

"Elliot, I was in and out."

"But you still had enough time to cut a deal with ABC . . . are you suicidal? You brought in that low life Miles Farmer, that pimp, and slapped your own production company in the face."

"How could I hurt *Lamplighter*? It runs like a dream, with or without me."

And Jocko hung up, thought of the roses that would rot without Katinka Baer.

He had no strategies, no real plan. He could hire someone to break Miles' legs, but that wouldn't bring him closer to Katinka. Yet he wasn't idle. His old man kept getting lost in the building, and Jocko had to pretend to be a trapper and a scout. Once, after he and Alfonso had made a futile search, and he considered bringing in the police, his dad arrived at the penthouse door with Katinka. She'd found him in the laundry room, had invited him up to her apartment to play pinochle and have some tea.

Jocko couldn't explain his own hunger. How could he be in love with a girl he'd met for five minutes, had pulled out of the snow? She wasn't wearing her gold-rimmed glasses, and Katinka had to squint.

"I thought you were away," Jocko said. "That's what Miles told me. We were—"

"I'm crazy about that thing on your scalp. It's like a shooting star."

"Yeah," Jocko muttered with a bitter smile. "I was shot in the head."

"It's the first thing I noticed . . . when you rescued me."

His dad fell asleep in a chair. Katinka took Jocko's hand, led him into his bedroom, as if she'd had her own floor plan. She started to undress. She had the same parrot on her shoulder that was like some logo from the Elephant's Hide. She was built like a child with breasts. And the musk of her body unsettled him. It was like a perfume that could rock him out of his long, terrible sleep, but Jocko wasn't sure that he wanted to wake up.

There was nothing violent or angular in her gestures. She could have been part of Jocko's particular dream. That's how she moved under him, as if they were voyaging together on a very narrow bed that could have been a canal.

They fell asleep, holding each other tight, but Katinka wasn't there when he woke. And Jocko was alone in his bedroom, like an abandoned child.

Inertia

6

Was it Dayton, Ohio? She couldn't remember. She'd carry a little mask on the plane, nod off as soon as her head touched the pillow, while one of the girls whispered in her ear. "Darling, don't dream too hard. You'll fall down a well and we'll never find you." She was born in a well, a black well that delivered blood. But somebody always found her.

They traveled en masse, like a battalion that was prepared to hit the beach of some new Normandy. Nothing got in their way. The girls could wreck a village, ruin an entire town. But they were becoming notorious, and they had to seek out hotels that were next to the airport, so they could vanish before the police arrived.

They'd booked into a businessman's convention, built their own little catwalk, where they could dance and model clothes. The clothes weren't for sale. They wore turbans to entice a customer, get a man to talk, not about his sexual preferences. They couldn't care less. They cared about mortgages, money in the bank. But Katinka had a lulu in this airport hotel. The lulu was in love with her. His name was Karl, and he owned a shoe factory in Detroit.

"Couldn't I visit you, Inertia? Or fly you in? I'm serious."

He'd finished a bottle of pink champagne. They were in the shoeman's suite. Katinka was bored. She wanted to scream. She could see the lights of the runway outside Karl's window. The lights seemed to ride out into infinity, like a mirage of blinking crosses. And Katinka wished she could plunge into that mirage, lose herself and Karl.

"I could give you an apartment on the top floor of my factory. No questions asked."

"Karl, I'm ashamed of you. Is that where you take your tricks?"

"I've never brought a woman within a mile of Sunshine Shoes. I don't fall in love that easily."

"I was on a platform, Karl. With twelve other females. They smiled at you. I didn't."

"You're the one," he said. "You're the one with class."

The shoeman had watched her dance for ten minutes. He'd sent a note to her with five hundred-dollar bills. *Must see you. Karl Sunshine, shoe manufacturer. I'm very serious.*

She couldn't tear up the note. The other girls had read it, and they might have tattled on Katinka. And so she met the shoeman, with the acid aroma of klieg lights on her, the sweat of her dance.

"I looked at you," he said, "and it was all over."

"Karly, what if I told you that I was a little murderess and a thief?"

"It wouldn't matter," he said. "I'll cure you."

"And suppose I didn't want to be cured?"

"I'd cure you anyway."

Lulus like that always hooked onto her. Did they discover their own isolation in her green eyes?

"Inertia, I have to make it clear. I'm not interested in a one-night stand."

"Neither am I," she said.

"And you couldn't model for other men."

"But that's my bread and butter."

"My accountant will take care of that. You'll be on my payroll."

"While I live near the roof? But what if I walked down one flight . . . into your factory?"

"I answer to no one," the shoeman said. "Walk wherever you like."

There was a knock on the door. The shoeman gathered his bathrobe around his neck. "Go away."

But the knocking only grew louder.

"Go away," the shoeman rasped. "I'll call the manager. We don't want to be disturbed."

And when the knocking persisted, the shoeman pulled a dart out of his briefcase. The dart was as long as an ice pick and had a beautiful feather at its blunted end. The shoeman pinched the dart with two fingers and shouted at the door.

"I won't be responsible if . . ."

A soldier with gray hair and Katinka's green eyes

marched into the room. The shoeman shivered, and the soldier plucked the dart out of his hand.

"Sunshine," the soldier said, "I'd like a little privacy."

"But this is my suite. I rented it."

"Did you rent my daughter too?"

"Daughter? I don't . . ."

"Sunshine, I'll count to three. And if you haven't locked yourself inside the bathroom, I'll take that dart and carve another hole in your ass."

"Careful, I have connections in Detroit. The king of the underworld. Carelli. I supply all his mistresses with shoes."

"Call him," the soldier said. "Right now. Tell him you're with Sergeant Baer."

"You couldn't possibly . . ."

"Sergeant Baer."

The shoeman locked himself inside the bathroom, and the soldier tossed the dart at Katinka. She wouldn't duck. The dart landed an inch from her ear. She had to clutch her thumbs to keep from crying.

"Daddy, he's the easiest mark I ever had."

"Who?"

"Sunshine. We could take him to the cleaner's."

"Why are you whispering?"

"He's in the toilet, daddy. He could have his ear to the door."

"Sunshine," the soldier shouted, "are you listening to this conversation?"

"No, sir," the shoeman said. And the soldier slapped Katinka's face.

"I have to track you to this fleabag, fly across the world. Tinka, you failed me. The Lamplighter shouldn't have survived a night with you. That was our bargain."

"Half the building would have known all about it."

"Known about what? You're as invisible as you want to be. His old man is forgetful. He would have blamed it on some drugged-out burglars."

"Who dance into a building with a day-and-night doorman?"

The soldier plucked the dart out of the wall and brushed Katinka's eye with its feather.

"Bitch," he said. "Can't even fuck that poor soul without feeling sorry for him. Or does the little dent in his skull turn you on? You could have strangled him in his sleep."

"Not until I strangle you."

He laughed, but his eyes wouldn't warm. "Tinka, I'd like it so much I'd have a hard-on, and my own dick would wake me up."

She wanted to grab the dart and stick it between his eyes. Whatever mayhem she'd done was only practice for her father's death.

The soldier shoved the dart into his pocket. "If you disappoint me, Tinka, you know what I'll do."

And he left the shoeman's suite, whistling to himself. She knocked on the bathroom door.

"Karly," she said, "come out, come out, wherever you are."

7

Jocko couldn't tear through the building like a rogue elephant, looking for a lost girl. He was the landlord's son. He sat down with his dad, played a hand of pinochle. Old Mr. Robinson began to cry.

"I'd rather play with Tinka. She smiles. Tinka makes me glad."

"And what am I?"

"You . . . you're a prisoner of war, occupying your old bedroom. I ought to charge you rent."

"How much would you like, dad? Ten thousand dollars a day?"

"Don't insult your old man."

"She's been here before, hasn't she, dad? In this apartment."

"Tinka? Why not? I can have visitors."

Jocko started to brood, and Mr. Robinson demolished him, cashed in his aces and kings. Jocko did feel like a prisoner of war. He wanted to question Alfonso about Katinka, but he didn't. He sat in his bedroom, like some man under house arrest. He forgot to shave. He watched reruns of *Lamplighter.* And then, one night, he put on his coat and went down to Wooster Street. That thick blue air of the Elephant's Hide was unbreathable. But Jocko hadn't come to breathe. He couldn't find Katinka, but Alfonso was sitting at the bar, surrounded by girls with tattoos on their shoulder. He wasn't dressed like a male nurse. Alfonso wore a black-leather coat at the Elephant's Hide, and silver bracelets. And now Jocko understood why Katinka had been so familiar with his bedroom. It wasn't her first visit. Alfonso had made love to her in Jocko's old room, had bit into her flesh. Jocko was convinced of that. He walked up to the bar, wedged himself between Alfonso and one of the girls.

He could see a flick of terror in Alfonso's eyes, under the nurse's grin.

"Alfonso," he whispered, "tell your old buddy, were you living with Tinka in my room before I arrived?"

He pounced on Alfonso, cracked him across the face, and the nurse continued to smile. Jocko didn't get the chance to hit him again. The cabaret's two bouncers grabbed Jocko by the collar and flung him into the street.

Jocko didn't even have the comfort of snow under his ass. Living in L.A. for so long had confused his calendar. He forgot that winter had already fled from the streets.

Alfonso didn't come back to work. But it wouldn't have mattered. Jocko tossed out his things, had them sent to the Elephant's Hide with a fat check. But he didn't know what to do about his dad, who kept whimpering, asking for his nurse. And then a man arrived out of nowhere, John Robevitch, a retired cop with a hearing aid. This Robevitch looked more desperate than Jocko's dad. He was Mr. Robinson's pinochle partner. Robinson and Robevitch. Jocko was immediately suspicious. Had Alfonso sent Robevitch around? But the ex-dick had entered Mr. Robinson's life long before Alfonso. He'd investigated a robbery in the building, and that's how he'd met old man Robinson. Jocko was still reluctant, but he hired Robevitch.

Mr. Robinson laughed a lot around his new nurse. Jocko had never been able to make the old man laugh. He learned to confide in Robevitch, and Robevitch asked him about his gloomy face.

"Ah." Jocko said. "It's ridiculous. I fell in love with a phantom."

Robevitch tapped his hearing aid, and Jocko had to repeat himself. "A phantom."

"It's not so ridiculous. I spent half my life chasing phantoms. That's the territory of a cop."

"But you must have solved thousands of cases."

"Yeah, when I bumped into somebody else's luck. Tell me about this phantom . . . is it a lady?"

"A girl," Jocko said. "A model who never made it. Katinka Baer. She's a nomad. But sometimes she sleeps in the building, with a couple of other models. They have their own little commune on the fourth floor."

Robevitch smiled. "Then let's have a look."

They avoided the elevator, took the stairs. Robevitch knocked on the models' door, and when no one answered he picked the lock with a pair of metal pins. Jocko had never seen a man with such nimble fingers. He was beginning to like Robevitch.

There wasn't a single picture on any of the walls. They were all nomads, Katinka's pals. Jocko couldn't even find a coffee pot. But there were closets and closets of clothes. Robevitch walked into one of the closets, then reappeared.

"It's phony," he said.

"What?"

"Nobody lives here."

"But how can you be so sure?"

Robevitch gave Jocko a gentle shove, got him out of the apartment. "A million dresses and shoes, but not one stinking pair of underpants. Nobody lives here."

It was Jocko who ended up watching his dad, because the retired cop was on a new case. Robevitch didn't have to travel with a gun; he had his lock picks and his hearing aid. "It's a hothouse," he said about the apartment on the fourth floor, "a watering hole."

"Robevitch, will you talk my language? I'm not the captain of your precinct."

The old detective seemed hurt. "You're a writer. Use your imagination."

"I'm lazy," Jocko said. "I've been living off one show."

"Then I'll lead you by the hand. The babes don't live in that apartment. It's their watering hole. It's where they crash when they have to crash, it's where they keep their clothes."

"Robevitch, I'm not that interested in their lives. I'm only interested in Katinka Baer."

"Sonny, it's the same subject."

"Just find her schedule. Clear up that one little mystery, will ya?"

The old detective was gone for six days. Jocko had to become his father's full-time keeper. He would venture into Washington Square Park with his dad. The days were much longer, but they didn't have that crystalline light without the snow. Jocko loved the barren winter trees, the frozen ground, and now the park was like a "hothouse" full of leaves.

He couldn't play pinochle in the park; all the tables were occupied with chess maniacs, wizards who sat for hours in front of a board, contemplating one or two moves. Jocko admired their devotion, that ability to let their minds dance on the diagonals of a chessboard, over and over again.

Robevitch returned with Katinka's itinerary.

"You're a magician, John. Where'd you get it?"

"From your television partner, Mr. Miles."

"Did you have to slap him around?" Jocko asked, his eyes on Robevitch's hearing aid.

"Never even met the man. I broke into his desk . . . but take my advice. Forget about this Katinka Baer. She's no phantom lady. She's very, very real. Your Tinka's involved in some big-time confidence crap."

But Jocko grabbed the itinerary, saw the words *Marseilles*, *Nice*, and *Menton* at the top of the page, and began to scratch his mind for some travel agent he could trust.

8

Sunshine.

She couldn't even slip away from a lousy shoeman. He'd left his wife and children to follow Katinka. He wore winter clothes on the Promenade des Anglais, like a polar bear who'd come drifting in from the arctic. She was having tea outside the Negresco. She couldn't go into the hotel. All the managers would have recognized Katinka. "Kate Moss," they called her, "Kate Moss with tits." She'd been fleecing customers for years, delicately, without much greed, until the Negresco caught on and flung Katinka out the back door. And so she'd have tea on the terrace, all alone. Katinka had escaped the little sisters of her clan, but she couldn't escape Sunshine Shoes.

"Karly," she said. "You're standing in my light. Sit down and I'll buy you a slice of rum cake."

"I'm broke," he said. "A truck arrived in the middle of the night, stole all my furniture and my goods.

I couldn't even collect on my insurance claim. The company said it had never seen a robbery like that, where everything was cleaned out, including the toilet paper. They wouldn't honor my claim. And then money disappeared from my bank account . . . I'm flat broke."

"How'd you find me?"

"Through my underworld connections."

"What connections?"

"Carelli. He owns Detroit. He told me about your father, awful things."

"And you've come to take revenge."

"No. I just want to be near you, Inertia."

"Karl, how much stupider can you get? I'm with my father's band. We're vultures . . . we already robbed you blind."

"Don't care."

He started to blubber. Katinka ordered tea and cake. He gobbled the rum cake in a single bite.

"Kiddo, do you have a place to sleep?"

He shrugged his shoulders.

"Come with me." Katinka took the polar bear by the hand to her headquarters on the Avenue des Fleurs. It was a pink house with a shield of palm trees that could have been lifted from Santa Monica or Miami. Sunshine entered the house and discovered a wonderland of girls, wearing Sunshine shoes. Alfonso was with the girls.

"Tinka, why'd you bring this fish? Get rid of him, or I will."

"Karl's my responsibility," Katinka said. "He'd still be solvent if he hadn't bumped into me."

"I'll cry for him," Alfonso said. "But it's dangerous to hang on to a fish we've already hooked."

"Why? Karl can be our catcher."

"What the hell do you mean?"

"He'll catch for us, do errands, grab our clothes when we have to run."

"We don't need an errand boy."

Katinka looked past Alfonso and his grim eyes. "Yes we do."

"For Christ's sake, he'll trip us up. He's a loser. Look at him."

"I like Karl," said Skeleton, Katinka's ally. "You heard Tinka. He'll catch for us."

"I say he goes."

The shoeman turned from face to face. He was overwhelmed, utterly confused. Inertia and her friends had eaten up his capital and his goods. And now his most aristocratic line had popped up like little rising submarines on the Avenue des Fleurs, in Nice. It wasn't fair, but he had to confess that he liked the way these corrupt girls modeled his shoes.

Alfonso took a piece of rope out of a drawer and knotted it into a leash. "He'll have to wear this."

"He's not a dog," said Skeleton. "Don't pick on Karl."

"He's weird," said Alfonso. "He'll call attention to us, and attention isn't what we need right now. We're walking on cracked ice . . ."

"There is no ice in Nice," said Karl.

Alfonso whacked him with the noose he'd just knotted. There was a red burn on Karl's cheek.

"Sunshine," Alfonso said, "you'll have to listen to me."

But the girls jumped on Alfonso, took away his leash, bound him head to toe, while Katinka dug the heel of her shoe into Alfonso's forehead.

"What's Karl's situation, huh?"

"Karl's our catcher," Alfonso said.

9

Jocko played the fox. He was planning to catch Katinka in Menton. She wasn't at her hotel on the Promenade du Soleil. He was about to leave when he saw Katinka on the wall, advertising "Hurricane Ladies, *une compagnie americaine,*" with its own traveling fashion show. But there wasn't a time or a date. And when he asked the hotel manager about these Ladies, all Jocko got was a grin.

"Haven't they been booked?"

"Certainly, Monsieur. But we aren't in a hurry."

La Princesse de Galles was a hotel for pensioners, a retirement inn. And Jocko was like a kindergartner in the lobby. He could comb the Riviera, searching for models with a parrot on their shoulder, but he decided to wait at La Princesse de Galles.

His room was splendid. It had two large windows that looked onto the sea and was much nicer than his bedroom in Manhattan or his cottage near Muscle Beach. He shopped on the Avenue Félix Faure, bought a sun helmet, sandals, and swimming trunks, but it was a little too cold to swim. He returned to the hotel, switched on his giant TV, and looked into the eyes of Byron Little. *Lamplighter* had come to Menton.

There was no sign of Katinka and her *"compagnie americaine."* The days grew warmer, and Jocko began to see swimmers outside his window. He went down to the hotel's private beach in his sandals, his helmet, and his trunks. While he lay in the sand, a parrot flew in front of his eyes. He looked up, saw one of the girls from the Elephant's Hide in a red bikini.

"Are you Skeleton?" he asked. "Or Midnight? Where's Inertia?"

But the girl wouldn't answer him. She ran off the beach. Jocko grabbed his sandals and his sun helmet and followed her into town. She climbed up into the Vieille Ville. He lost her somewhere in those twisted streets, found her again as she entered a narrow door on the Montée du Souvenir. He was about to catch her when a hand hauled him into the same little house.

He stood in a dark room that was barely as tall as Jocko himself. The girl was gone. Alfonso, his dad's old keeper, was aiming a gun at him. Jocko's heart didn't even pound.

"I died once. I can die again."

"It's not a joke. You shouldn't have asked about Katinka. We can't open with you around. You're a lovesick groupie. You'll leave a trail."

"I'm not a groupie," Jocko said. "And I don't give a fuck about your fashion show. I want Katinka."

Alfonso leered at him. "Tinka doesn't want you."

Alfonso shouldn't have been so careless with the gun. Jocko slapped it out of his hand, scooped it off the stone floor, and dug it between Alfonso's temples.

"I'm staying. Menton's mine."

He walked out onto the Montée du Souvenir, climbed down the hill, and flung Alfonso's gun into the green sea . . .

He swam, brought bottles of coffee to the beach. No more parrots flew across his blanket-towel. But there was bedlam in the lobby. The *"compagnie americaine"* had come to town. They didn't have a proper runway; the girls had to do their strut on a thick red carpet. There was no order or reason in their entrances and exits. They were like unconscious animals from a chaotic zoo. Their trainer was Alfonso, who wore a sequined outfit that glorified his biceps and his back. He crooned into a microphone while the Hurricane Ladies marched. They must have been their own couturiers. They'd dressed themselves as harlequins and little girls. One of them wore a mustache. They'd painted their bodies, pierced their navels, wore chains around their bellies. And Katinka was among them, half blind without her gold-rimmed glasses; pale-green eyes fluttering against the brutal lobby lights. She was in a boy's polo shirt, with a kerchief masking her breasts. She had short shorts and low leather boots, like some Little Orphan Annie who'd suffered a strange, explosive puberty.

The pensioners couldn't take their eyes off "Inertia." They loved her *défilé*. It wasn't Seventh Avenue, or the catwalks of Paris and Milan. It was a dreamy bathhouse hotel near the beaches of Menton. But Jocko couldn't get beyond the bedlam. Even with her blindness, Katinka hadn't looked at him once.

"Tinka," he said, stepping in front of her like a cat.

But she steered around Jocko, as if he were one more pensioner at La Princesse de Galles.

And then, in the middle of the night, she appeared outside Jocko's door in her boy's polo shirt, with blue paint on her nose.

"Mr. Lamplighter, aren't you going to let me in?"

Jocko could almost taste the gin on her tongue. She walked into the room, sat on Jocko's bed, toppled over, fell asleep.

He was sitting next to her when she woke. She had a crazed look in her eye.

"Get out of here," she said. "Alfonso warned you once."

"Ah," he said, "I'm interfering with the animal trainer."

She slapped his face. He grabbed her arms, shook Katinka.

"What else should I call him? He took you into the penthouse. Don't deny it. You slept with that son of a bitch . . . in my bed."

The crazed look was gone. The harder Jocko shook her, the harder she laughed.

"Idiot," she said. "I wouldn't let Alfonso touch me. I did a fashion show."

"For whom?" Jocko had to ask.

"Your dad. He liked to watch me model clothes."

"You did a lousy striptease for my dad?"

"You can call it that."

"And was Alfonso there?"

"Naturally . . . Mr. Robinson wouldn't have had any fun without him."

She pulled away from Jocko and bolted out of the room.

10

Karl was the catcher. He wore a clown's costume, with big shoes and a painted face. He was in love with Inertia, desperately in love, and when she performed on the runway at this senior-citizens' hotel, he was jealous of whoever gazed at her, looked at her too long. Sunshine had never felt such rage. He wasn't a shoeman anymore. He'd stopped caring about his fall and winter line. His only season was Inertia. He gave up the dream of ever sleeping with her, of becoming her pirate, an ex-shoeman from Detroit, who'd paid through the nose for sex outside his meager marriage. He could bear the humility of it all, the pain, if Inertia was also celibate, if Inertia lived like a nun. But there was a man at the hotel, a billionaire, Alfonso said, a nabob who'd been chasing Inertia across the planet, like Sunshine himself. Sunshine had read about him in the *Wall Street Journal*. Jocko Robinson, the creator of Byron Little and all the other Lamplighters, who were the princes and princesses of Detroit. *Lamplighter* had destroyed Sunshine Shoes' bargain-hunter Tuesday nights. Detroit became a ghost town while Byron Little was on the air. Even Carelli, the crime lord, wouldn't stir from his television set, which was the size of a wall. And Sunshine would have to attend the marathon sessions at Carelli's house, because the crime lord needed all his cronies around him, and the man who supplied his mistresses with shoes. Carelli had grown fond of Karl, or he would have seized Sunshine Shoes and turned it into a pizza parlor. But he loved having a shoeman with a bachelor's degree from Wayne State.

The crime lord himself could have been a Lamplighter. He was a violin prodigy at the age of six. But he'd come down with German measles, which ravaged his body, scarred him, and made him deaf in one ear. His dad was a burglar who sang at weddings and was killed in a minor mob war. And the little stunted musician rose out of the streets with his deaf ear and took over Detroit before he was thirty. He had three sons, none of whom could ever master the violin. He wept in front of the tube, because Byron Little was also an ex-prodigy, who'd been stung by a bee and endured a mild paralysis in his playing hand.

"Mr. Sunshine," Carelli said, "it's the story of my life . . . talent gone to waste. I could have been another Heifetz. And look at me now? I frighten people. Call that a profession? I should be playing Brahms."

"Certainly." Sunshine said. "Brahms."

"Don't patronize me, Shoeman," the crime lord hissed, and pulled a dart with a green feather out of a gorgeous wooden box. "I could shove this between your eyes, and it would be the end of the world . . . but here, take it as a gift from Carelli. You could pulverize a man with a dart like that."

It was the same sleek dart that Sunshine had lost to the soldier, Inertia's dad. Carelli would never forgive him. The dart had come from the priceless collection of an Italian duke. Carelli bought out the duke's entire castle. It softened the pain of his brittle ear, lent him the illusion of a noble lineage. And poor Sunshine couldn't even hold on to an aristocrat's dart. But there it was on a bench in Menton, waiting for him, with the green feather and the pristine point.

"You know what to do with it, Karly."

Alfonso had crept up behind him.

"Jocko's gonna steal Inertia for himself. You'll be nothing, Karl."

"He can't . . ."

"Go up to his room, Karl."

"I'm afraid. I'll wet my pants . . . he's the Lamplighter."

"He's a dime a dozen. He was shot in the head. You'll be doing him a favor. You'll end his misery, Karl."

"I can't."

"And what will it be like without Inertia? You'll waste away, Karl. You'll shrink."

"But I've never . . ."

"Do it. One jolt in the neck, and Inertia is yours."

Sunshine was like a sleepwalker. He wandered into La Princesse de Galles, went up to Robinson's room. He had a key in his hand. Alfonso must have planted it on him. Sunshine opened the door. He didn't hate the Lamplighter. Perhaps he could plead with him, beg the nabob to go away . . . without Inertia.

But he was clutching the dart, Carelli's dart. He saw himself in the mirror. He was smiling now. He was the catcher, capable of killing a man . . .

And then he felt a thwack on his jaw. The Lamplighter must have overpowered him. The Lamplighter was an invisible man.

"Karly . . ."

Sunshine was lying on the floor.

Inertia stood above him, with the dart and the key.

"I saw you on the promenade. Did Alfonso sing in your ear?"

"He said the Lamplighter would kidnap—"

"Karl, did you promise to catch for us?"

"I did. But what's the point?"

"The point is that we're leaving Menton."

"With the Lamplighter?"

"Karly, did you ever see me look at another man?"

"But they all look at you."

"That doesn't give them the right of possession. How can we leave if you won't catch for us, pack our bags? And if you come into a man's room, any man's room, with a dart, I'll kill you myself, Karly, hear?"

He started to cry. "Yes, Inertia."

"We need you, Karl. You're one of us."

"Yes, Inertia."

She whisked him out of the room, and he started to catch for the Hurricane Ladies, started to carry down their trunks, like an educated mule, while Katinka captured Alfonso.

"Darling," she said, "you'd better sleep with a nice big brace around your neck, because I'm in a murderous mood."

"Tinka, I'm only following orders."

"Karly's our catcher, not yours. And if the police grab him, we're out of business, and that includes you."

"But we can retire, once Jocko's gone."

"Retire to what? The fattest jail in France. Jocko's our lucky star . . . our Lamplighter."

"Your dad doesn't think so."

"My dad's a psychotic prick . . . now should we wait for the police, or ride the hell out of here?"

"Ride," Alfonso said. "But couldn't I keep the dart?"

"Not unless you want it tacked onto your anatomy."

And Alfonso scrambled into his room, leaving her to think about that billionaire with the mark of a pig's tail on his head.

The Dom

11

He was resting in the sand, with his sun helmet, reading *The Last Tycoon,* when a pair of policemen crept up on him. They weren't rude with Jocko, weren't aggressive, like the flics of L.A., who'd impose their importance on you until you believed that your whole life was a major crime. These two flics didn't even ask Jocko to get dressed. He walked with them in his sandals and trunks to the *commissariat* on the other side of the hotel.

The *commissaire*'s name was Bertrand. He asked questions about Byron Little. All the flics of Menton watched *Lamplighter* religiously. The *commissaire* had lived in Chicago once. He spoke English like one of the reformed thugs on *Lamplighter.* He had a big nose and big hands and such broad, theatrical gestures that Jocko wondered if Cyrano de Bergerac might have been reborn in Menton as a flic.

"These mannequins, Monsieur Robinson, they are very bad girls."

Jocko liked the police chief. He didn't want to lie. But he couldn't trap Katinka, no matter what she'd done. "They're not really friends of mine, Commissaire."

"You arrived before they did. You asked about one of the mannequins, a certain Katinka Baer. Were you casing the town for them, like the little fish who arrive before the sharks?"

"What have they done, Commissaire?"

"Nothing definitive. But there have been robberies during their stay in Menton, strange robberies . . . missing necklaces, missing rings, cash boxes that were opened quite mysteriously. And we cannot find much information about the Hurricane Ladies . . . mannequins without a history. The hotel hired them because they were quite cheap. I'm still curious. You're a rich man. Why would you front for such miserable sharks?"

Jocko looked into the *commissaire*'s eyes. "I'm in love with Katinka." He fished a checkbook out of his trunks. "What's the damage, Commissaire?"

"Damage?"

"Yes. Whatever's been stolen. I'll pay for it. In dollars or francs."

He could have had his own bar stool at La Princesse de Galles. The flics saluted him and the pensioners recognized Jocko as the one and only dad of Byron Little and all the other Lamplighters. He could escape lawyers and writer-producers, but not the relentless echo of a murder-mystery show. The maids began to look at Jocko with some kind of awe, as if he could breathe fire, turn them into Lamplighters or singing ostriches and philosophical kings. He'd become the magician of Menton.

He couldn't go into a restaurant without scribbling his autograph or posing with the chef. He had to withdraw from the world of Menton, take his meals in his own room. He wouldn't answer the phone. He sat in his tub, without the sun helmet.

There was a knock on his door.

"Scram," he screamed.

Cyrano de Bergerac entered the room with his own key. "Dear friend," said the chief of police. "I worry about you. I will have to ask you to leave Menton."

"I haven't committed a crime," Jocko said. "And you can't link me to the Hurricane Ladies."

"But that is the problem. You'll shrivel up and shrink if you wait too long. Your fiancée is in Cologne."

"I don't have a fiancée."

"Monsieur Jocko, my men have worked like dogs. Don't make little of us. You've paid the mannequins' bills. I've refunded all the wounded parties. And I'm not obligated to notify the German police . . . now save yourself. I insist."

12

It was a cathedral with two burnt towers. The Dom. It had survived constant American and British bombings, like a singular orphan, while the rest of Cologne had become a huge gray field. And the city that Jocko saw from his window at the Dom Hotel had risen right out of the ruins like a miraculous living cake. But he was still confused. Cologne hadn't been on the inventory that Robevitch, the deaf detective, had stolen from Miles Farmer's desk. Katinka shouldn't have come to Cologne, according to the list.

Jocko went to Old Market Square, had coffee and a slice of Black Forest cake. Then he walked to the Rhine, sat down near the water, silvered by the sun. Two men came up behind him, lifted Jocko off his bench. They had broken noses and cauliflower ears, like comical prizefighters. Alfonso Walsh was with them, carrying an enormous pair of scissors. While the cauliflower men held his arms, Alfonso cut the pockets out of Jocko's pants, with his wallet, his cash, his credit cards.

"I warned you, but you wouldn't listen."

"I'm your angel," Jocko said. "I settled your account in Menton. The police chief isn't even looking for the Ladies."

"Prick, he sent you here."

Alfonso socked him three times, and as he began to fall the cauliflower men kicked at him; Jocko had to clutch his groin.

He returned to the Dom Hotel in his mutilated pants, called Santa Monica, got his banker out of bed. "You're cracking up," Elliot Weinrib muttered, but Jocko didn't have to worry. An envelope arrived at the hotel in two hours with twenty thousand dollars' worth of deutsche marks . . .

He bought a fresh pair of pants on Cologne's High Street, covered the bumps on his face with mercurochrome, and then he was fine. He loved to hear the Dom's big bell. It was the heaviest bell in the world, with a huge metal tongue and scaffolding to support the bell tower. The sound of the bell would break into your dreams, and you could feel all of Cologne tremble under your feet. Jocko wondered how he had ever survived without the ringing of the Dom.

He was having breakfast at the hotel, drinking tons of peppermint tea, when he saw the same two cauliflower men. Jocko's first instinct was to protect the pockets of his pants. The cauliflower men arrived at Jocko's table, returned his wallet, his credit cards, and his cash. Then they disappeared and another man arrived. He also had a broken nose, but there was nothing comical about him. He wore a beautiful white turtleneck and a silk jacket. He sat down next to Jocko, barked in German to the breakfast waiter, who brought him rolls in a blue basket and a pot of peppermint tea. He introduced himself, held out his paw to Jocko.

"Lothar Schill. I apologize. There's been a mistake. Those clowns who kicked you are on my payroll. It's not their fault. Alfonso poisoned their minds. And no one told me that Herr Lamplighter was in town."

"I'm not the Lamplighter," Jocko said. "And Byron Little is a fucking cliché."

"You're modest," said Lothar Schill, "and a little angry with me. But I beg you to come to my café. You won't be disappointed. Der Papagei, on Martinstrasse. You can't miss it."

He finished his tea and was gone.

"Who is that guy?" Jocko asked the breakfast waiter.

"Him?" the waiter said. "Herr Lothar. The King of Cologne."

13

Suddenly, like a crooked spear that had entered his heart, Sunshine began to miss Detroit. He couldn't understand a continent where dollars bloomed into deutsche marks, and "Mister" became *Mein Herr*. He never got to see the sun. He had to dress and undress the Hurricane Ladies, rinse glasses behind a bar, watch Inertia dance with other men . . . until Detroit itself walked into Sunshine's daydreams. Carelli. The crime lord appeared in a winter coat of lamb's wool.

"Mr. Carelli, what are you doing in Cologne?"

"Pretending to be a tourist," Carelli said, watching Katinka dance.

"Then you know Inertia . . . and her dad?"

"Sunshine, what can I say? I met her when she was a tomboy. Tinka's almost my niece."

"I never harmed you, Mr. C. I outfitted all your women. And you broke Sunshine Shoes."

"It was an accident, I swear. Like salt in your eye.

You shouldn't have connected with these ladies. They're diabolical. They work for me . . . and Lothar Schill."

"Inertia isn't diabolic."

"Sunshine, never trust a tomboy. But I won't leave you stranded. You'll draw a salary. You're on my personal payroll."

"Can I wear a gun?"

"What for?"

"So I can shoot the men who dance with Inertia."

"Shoeman, you'll be swimming in blood . . . no guns."

"Then use your power. Please. Rescue her. Scatter all the men before I go crazy."

"I'll do one better. I'll dance with her myself."

And he walked across the dark dance hall, stopped in front of Katinka, who was dancing with three sailors. The other girls saw Carelli, shivered, smiled, and pulled the sailors out of Katinka's arms.

"What gives?" Katinka growled. She saw Carelli and started to swoon. He caught her, and continued the dance.

"Kitten, aren't you gonna say hello?"

She came out of her stupor long enough to wink at him. But the left side of her face was completely frozen. Carelli was her father's closest ally, had served under him as a young recruit when Katinka was growing up in Bonn. Uncle Lionello. He was as rich as the Lamplighter. But Lionello's assets were undeclared. Lionello liked to play poor. He wouldn't even live in a mansion.

"I come to Cologne, and the first thing I see is Karl Sunshine. That's obscene. What's he doing in your entourage?"

"I adopted him. He showed up in Nice, at the Negresco, like some magic arrow had drawn him to us."

"That arrow was me. I had to help him out. But I was hoping you'd get rid of him. You had your instructions. He's penniless, Tinka."

"I'm not good at gold digging, Uncle. I never was."

"I could choke you right on this floor. No one would hear your death rattle."

"What?" Katinka said, half her face still frozen. "Destroy your godchild? Dad would haunt you the rest of your life."

"He'd rejoice," Carelli said. "I'd miss you more than he would."

"That's because you never slapped me enough."

"I helped raise you, remember?"

"But you didn't seem to mind having men kiss me before I was twelve."

"Your dad did most of the kissing. How could I stop him?"

"You were an angel, Lionello. I owe you my life."

Carelli stared at the dart in Katinka's hand. "That's an heirloom. I lent it to Sunshine."

"Dad took it from him. Then you had Alfonso give it back. You're always plotting murders, Lionello, like a Renaissance prince . . ."

A man in a red scarf came up to Lionello, drummed

him on the back with a finger. “Beg your pardon. May I have this dance?”

“I don’t dance with strangers,” Carelli said.

The man smiled. He had his own bodyguard. “It’s the young lady I want. Your Fräulein.”

“You can’t have her.”

“But she comes with the club. I was told that I could rent her.”

“They told you wrong.”

The man motioned to his bodyguard. “Burt, will you deal with this pest?”

Katinka tried to close her eyes. She knew what would happen next.

Lionello tapped the bodyguard with his knuckles and lunged at the man, took a bite out of his cheek.

The man in the red scarf screamed, and Lothar arrived in an instant, with a first-aid kit. He danced around Carelli, without disturbing him, took the man behind the bar, bathed his cheek in peroxide.

Katinka didn’t look back. She vanished from the dance hall with the dart still in her hand.

14

One evening, in the middle of a heat wave, Jocko wandered onto Martinstrasse, saw a neon sign outside Der Papagei. It was a blinking parrot that reminded him of the tattoos on the Hurricane Ladies. And Jocko cursed his own stupidity. He was the cliché, not Herr Lamplighter. All the models worked for Lothar.

He entered, saw the models drink and dance with customers. They weren't doing fashion tonight. There was no catwalk at Der Papagei. Katinka stood at the bar with Alfonso Walsh. She wore a dark suit that draped her figure like the scaffolding on the bell. She didn't turn toward him when he approached the bar, didn't say hello. But he twisted Alfonso around, tossed a dish of olives in his eyes, cracked him once, twice, and ran out of the cabaret . . .

He began to see little cauliflower men all over the place, as if the town were made of Lothar's minions. They didn't menace Jocko, didn't attack him once, just followed behind him, like a company of fools. The cauliflower men were there at breakfast, or close to the cathedral, listening to the bells. He couldn't buy a shirt or eat a meal without them. He understood the motive behind their repertory: the King wanted to drive him from Cologne.

He'd almost gotten used to the sons of bitches when an enormous Chrysler stopped for him near Alter Markt in the Old Town. The rear door opened, and Jocko got in, sat next to the King, who wore a red blazer. Alfonso was driving the car.

"Look what you did to my man," Lothar said, pointing to the bandages on Alfonso's forehead and cheeks,

"I could have done worse."

"Herr Lamplighter, we are all a family," said the King of Cologne. "We have to stick together."

"Is Katinka part of the family too?"

"She's like a daughter to me."

"What was she doing in Menton? The Ladies were only a cover. They didn't rob, they didn't steal. They didn't even go to bed with the chief of police. They just drew attention away from your real enterprises. Your little fucking men sacked half of Menton while the Ladies were around."

"It's nothing, a trick I learned from the Lamplighters."

"Yeah," Jocko said. "Tell me how *Lamplighter* has made you the master of crime."

Lothar started to laugh. "Why are you cruel to your own children?"

"They're not my children," Jocko said.

He leapt out of the car on Loreleystrasse and took a cab back to the hotel. His heart beat at an imbecilic pace. He was absolutely certain that Katinka was up in his room, waiting for him in some kind of gypsy outfit the King had chosen. The car ride had only been a ruse. The King was trying to choreograph Jocko's little romance.

But there wasn't even the ghost of Katinka in his room, not a hint of her perfume, not a gypsy hat on his bed. And Jocko began to feel like an orphan in Cologne.

He booked a seat on the next flight to Athens. He'd been so involved with *Lamplighter* before he was shot in the head that he missed his chance to see the Parthenon and all the other little cradles of the West. He'd visited Florence with an Italian producer, attended trade fairs in Barcelona and Berlin, but the Greek market wasn't big enough to have its own fair. And he never stood on the Acropolis with any Greek producer.

He could *feel* the Parthenon, see a broken temple on a great green hill. But he couldn't pack his suitcase, couldn't leave his room. He was waiting for Katinka.

He had lunch on his bed. He stopped shaving. He no longer listened to the Dom.

His door opened. He wondered if the cauliflower men had come to kill him. He wouldn't resist. Jocko coveted the dark. He wanted his coma again.

Several faces peered at him.

"Mein Herr?"

He recognized the manager and some guy with jug-handled ears. Elliot Weinrib. His banker was in Cologne. Elliot had flown in from Santa Monica just to greet him.

"Hiya, kid. Put on a shirt. I'm taking you home."

He couldn't remember much about the flight. He wore a blanket around his shoulders. And then Elliot brought him someplace. It wasn't Malibu. It wasn't Washington Square. He didn't even end up sleeping in his own bed. He wouldn't have minded Misericordia if he could have his old nurse . . . and bagels from Farmers Market. But the nurses here looked like bigger, stronger cauliflower men.

—Jocko, is that you?

He must have been in some playroom for grownups. Jocko noticed chessboards, a giant jungle gym. A man was next to him, a movie star, Matthew Pine, who'd been making three–four million a pop several years ago and suddenly disappeared from the circuit. He was a coprophiliac. A cameraman had discovered him on the set, playing with his own caca.

Matthew Pine lost his children. His wife kicked him out. But he'd been a fan of *Lamplighter* from the beginning, and he did a couple of guest appearances while he was still riding high, played "Oliver Grimm," an eccentric counterfeiter, and helped boost the ratings.

"Mat, where the hell are we?"

"Diamond House, a very private clinic."

"In Switzerland or what?"

The movie star laughed. "Yes, the Swiss canton of New Jersey . . . a hop and a skip from Manhattan."

"And how long have you been—"

"A guest at Diamond House? For centuries. Jocko, you'll love it here. I promise."

And he trounced Jocko in a game of chess.

15

There were no poor people at the clinic, just loony millionaires like Matthew and himself. And he wondered how much it was costing him to stay. He could dial long distance from his room, which sat over the Hudson and looked out onto the lights of lower Broadway. He caught Elliot at his firm, Weinrib and Salomon, a private banking house that paid all of Jocko's bills.

"Elliot, did my father sign the commitment papers?"

"There was nothing to sign. You can walk out of there. You're a free man."

"I don't believe it. The nurses have biceps like ostrich eggs."

"It's only an illusion, They're licensed therapists. I checked."

"But you still haven't told me the price tag."

"Two thousand and ten dollars a day, half of it picked up by your medical coverage."

"What about the other half?"

"If you're worried, we'll pull a chunk out of your pension plan. Now stop groaning and lemme get back to work."

Jocko had to test Elliot's theory. He waltzed right out of the clinic. None of the guards did a thing. He stood outside the gate, sucked half a cigarette, stared at the balconies and painted shutters of Diamond House, went back in, got involved in a game of magnetic darts with a muscle-bound nurse until he happened to see Matthew standing in a corner of the playroom with tears in his eyes.

He went over and put his arm around Mat. "What's wrong?"

"Dunno," said the movie actor. "I can't stop crying."

"Ah, it's only natural. You miss your wife and kids. You can't find your own history inside a clinic. Mat, we have to sneak out of here."

The movie actor wiped his eyes. "You can go. I'll live without my history."

He was on his magic mountain, the Jersey Palisades, and Jocko didn't have to consider the rest of the planet. He had his solitude until a nurse knocked on his door.

"Mr. Robinson, your bride is here . . . that's what she says. She's with a man."

The King had come with Katinka, who wore a wedding gown with a little white veil, her gold-rimmed glasses, and the same tattoo on her shoulder. The King was carrying goblets and a split of champagne. Jocko couldn't toss them out of the clinic. They were his guests. He walked them into his room, closed the door.

"This isn't funny."

Lothar handed him a goblet and poured the champagne. "Mensch, why did you abandon us?"

"This isn't funny."

"It's a ritual. Every fashion show has to have a bride."

"Are you performing at the clinic?"

"Herr Lamplighter, we're performing for you."

And the King vanished with his goblet. Jocko was terrified. Katinka sipped champagne under her veil and started to undress.

"No," Jocko said. "I'm not like my dad . . . I don't need fashion shows."

"What do you need?" she asked, with one long furl of her pale-green eyes.

"I need," Jocko muttered, "I need you not to be my trick."

"I'm not tricking," Katinka said. "You're my hero. You saved me from the snow."

"Let me buy you back from the King. I don't care about the price. You won't have to wear a veil anymore."

"I love my veil. And Lothar isn't my pimp."

"I could lend you a little money. No strings attached. You can stop dancing and stripping for old men."

"And start stripping for you. You want to make me into your private princess . . . well, should I dress or undress?"

Jocko ripped off her bridal veil. She blinked at him, hurled champagne into his eyes. "No strings attached." She ran out of the room and off Jocko's mountain with the King of Cologne.

The Elephant's Hide

16

Mr. Robinson mourned his dead mistresses and his dead wife. He was too old to voyage out of the building and find another mistress. What would he do with her? Play poker or Scrabble? He had a peanut in his pants. There were no miracle drugs for Mr. Robinson. He'd been a scoundrel, had lusted everywhere . . . when he could lust. He'd kept women in the building while his wife was around, squirreled them away on different floors. He'd neglected Jocko, who was a witness to his perfidies and machinations. It was like having a grand inquisitor in the house. But Mr. Robinson's inquisitor was always silent. How did such a melancholy boy become a billionaire? Byron Little and the Lamplighters. Mr. Robinson despised the show, but he couldn't stop watching it. His silent son had invented a crooked ex-prosecutor whose only weapon was talk-talk-talk. Mr. Robinson had never seen Byron slap a woman or punch a man. Byron's constant gab was like sweet revenge on the old man: the "lamps" that Byron lit for the mob often involved women messengers who could have come out of Mr. Robinson's old harem. They were the doubles of Clara, Maxine, Louise . . . Mr. Robinson's mistresses. And he'd cry when he saw these messengers from hell, the little lamplighters who were desperately devoted to Byron. He'd talk back to the teli.

"Jocko, I loved your mom, not Clara . . ."

A shadow crept across the screen.

"Uncle Rob," the shadow said, "did you forget all about me?"

Mr. Robinson began to warble. "Tinka, is that you?"

"Who else would visit such a wicked old man?"

"Where have you been?"

"All over. Trying to save your son."

"He's not worth saving," Mr. Robinson said. "He invented Byron Little to eat my heart out."

"Byron's cute."

Mr. Robinson snapped off *Lamplighter* with his remote. "It's nothing, a rerun. I know it by heart. I could recite it for you, Tinka. Byron Little and the Gashouse Gang. He rescues Albany from the police."

"Chicago," Tinka said. "Albany doesn't have a Gashouse Gang."

"You're addicted, aren't you?"

"Everybody needs a guardian angel, Uncle Rob."

"Byron Little's a thief, an evil mastermind."

"That's the only kind that counts."

"Will you model for me, Tinka . . . take off your clothes?"

"I'm not in a modeling mood."

"We're old acquaintances . . . didn't I reduce your rent?"

"After I started stripping. Not before. And who leads you out of the basement when you get lost near the washing machines?"

"Model for me . . . I'll sign any document you want."

"No!"

John Robevitch had arrived. That pest. Mr. Robinson felt like banning him from the premises.

"Did I invite you here? I'm negotiating with Katinka."

"Then the negotiations are off . . . Robinson, she's an adventuress."

"But I like adventuresses, John."

"Your son is languishing. And she's responsible."

"Good for her . . . Tinka, you have my blessings."

But Tinka was already gone. Robevitch had chased her away with his recriminations. He should never have brought a detective into the house.

"I could kill you, John."

"Stop talking and put on your shoes."

"But I don't need shoes. I'm the landlord. I can wear slippers when I want. Why should I care what my tenants think of me?"

"I'm not worried about your tenants, Mr. R. Come on."

17

He was sitting in the playroom, staring at the wall, when a man with an odd little apparatus behind one ear entered Jocko's field of vision.

"Glad you could make it, John. Would you like to dance?"

"Shhh, sonny. The walls have ears."

Jocko looked at Robevitch's hearing aid and started to laugh.

"Where's dad? Did he find a new stripper to take Katinka's place?"

"Forget Katinka. Your dad's safe. I might not be able to kidnap you with him around."

"Kidnap me? Robevitch, I'm a free man."

"Someone's been selling you a song . . . get up slow, very slow, and follow me."

"Can't I say good-bye to my friend Matthew Pine?"

"The movie star?" Robevitch said. "Is he in this dungeon?"

Robevitch discovered Mat in the playpen, got his

autograph, and started to navigate Jocko closer and closer to the clinic's front door.

Two of the muscle-bound nurses blocked their exit.

"Who are you?" one of them bellowed. "You have no authority . . . Mr. Robinson is suffering from severe depression. He can't leave the grounds today."

Robevitch pulled a very small gun out of his pocket.

"I think I just cured him . . . get out of my way."

"Sir, we can't—"

"Don't test me. I have a short attention span." He shoved the gun into the same nurse's groin. "It might go off."

The two nurses stepped aside and Robevitch barreled through the front door with Jocko, brought him down to the taxi that was waiting near the gate. Jocko saw a figure through the glass. His dad was sitting in the rear like a bishop with a blanket on his knees. Mr. Robinson started to growl. "What took you so long? I was getting lonely."

The little detective was so absorbed, he almost forgot to collect Jocko from the clinic. "It's bunko from beginning to end. That lawyer of yours is behind it all. Elliot What's-his-face."

"Elliot Weinrib, and he isn't my lawyer."

"But he's still after your money."

"Don't be ridiculous . . . he's almost as rich as I am."

"Then why is he gobbling up property in your dad's name?"

"What property?"

"The Elephant's Hide . . . and that fancy prison on the Palisades."

"Dad owns Diamond House and a cabaret?"

"He doesn't own shit. What's-his-face collects all the fees. He has power of attorney. I can put out a contract on Elliot. I'm not kidding. I have very deep pockets inside the police."

"Jesus," Jocko said. "You sound just like Byron Little. I don't believe a thing. Let's kidnap Miles Farmer. That's a much more appealing project."

The little detective started to groan. "Farmer is nothing, half a peanut."

"But he knows a lot about Katinka."

"She's on Elliot's payroll. That's all we have to know."

"And you're on my payroll, John. I say we go for Miles."

But Miles was off the screen. Not even Robevitch's contacts could find him. He'd shut his office, didn't seem to have an address. Robevitch grew more and more irritable. "Sonny, the clock is ticking, and we've already wasted a week. Our enemies get stronger, and we sit around sucking our fingers."

"Miles will surface. He's not very good at playing dead."

18

Old man Robinson discovered Miles loitering in Washington Square, under the aegis of a false mustache, and lured him up to the penthouse.

Robevitch started to pummel Miles, rap him on the head. "Swear to me that Elliot Weinrib isn't your boss."

Miles clutched Jocko, cried into the pocket of his pants. "On my life. I don't know any Weinribs."

Robevitch ripped off the fake mustache. "Then we'll play a little game of suicide. I'll walk you to the window and—"

"Jocko," Miles said, "help me. I'm your writing partner."

"Then why did you close shop, decide to live without an address?"

"Because that rotten King came after me, with his battlers . . . ya know, his personal palookas from Cologne. The King says I gave you certain information, told you about his gig in Menton. He said

I had no future in Manhattan or anywhere else . . . Jocko, what about our deal with ABC? We have to develop a script. Perry Bowles called and called. I didn't have a clue where you were. I have bills to pay, and I lost my fax line."

"We'll get you another one. But tell me about the King and Katinka Baer."

"His green-eyed baby? He found her in Bonn. She was fourteen. Her dad was stationed there, in Bonn, I think. He's an American soldier who smuggled goods for the King, right out of the PX. They were partners, I think, until the King got too big. Or maybe her old man had money problems, and sold his little girl to the King."

"Say it," Jocko shouted. "Lothar is her pimp."

"No, no. They lived together. It was legit."

"But they're not living together now."

"That's romance," Miles said. "It comes and goes . . ."

Robevitch hit him again. "He's lying. He works for Weinrib."

Jocko had to grab Robevitch's fist out of the air. "Stop slapping him, John. This isn't a police station."

Miles continued to cry into Jocko's pants. "What'll we do? I can't stall Perry Bowles. We'll lose our ticket at ABC."

"Not to worry," Jocko said. "I'll take care of Bowles."

He was sitting beside the pool at the Chateau Marmont with Perry Bowles, lord of ABC. He would often hide out at the Chateau during his *Lamplighter* days, when he was in the thick of production and couldn't sleep, because Duck Soup was right down the hill, and if he got hungry, he could drink a pint of carrot juice at The Source.

"Forgive me," said Perry Bowles, "you're sitting in outer space, and I have to sell a show that doesn't have a title, or an outline, or a star."

"But we do have a star. Matthew Pine."

Jocko could hear Perry grind his jaw. "The caca man? I thought the show was about sexy models who live in a dump and protect old men from wise guys in the neighborhood."

"And don't they need somebody to protect *them*?"

"Matthew Pine. My lawyers will have a fit."

"He'll be perfect. A disgraced cop, without a pension, who's a kind of exalted janitor at the girls' building and is connected to all the wise guys . . . Perry, wouldn't you like to resurrect Matthew Pine? They'll love him in middle America. Movie star battles illness and prepares his comeback at ABC. Your sponsors won't be able to resist . . ."

Jocko saw a girl in a blue bikini and a white bathing cap at the other end of the pool. Sharon

Stone's pale sister, Florence Trout, with a parrot tattooed on her shoulder.

That pig's tail on Jocko's skull began to beat.

The lord of ABC babbled about Matthew Pine, but Jocko was no longer listening. He wondered if Duck Soup could lend him a gun.

19

All he had to do was wait. Florence Trout hadn't come to swim at the Chateau by chance. Elliot kept a bungalow for her at the Chateau Marmont, far from his wife and kids. That's how sure Elliot was of himself. He knew that Jocko loved the place, that it was Jocko's hideout in Hollywood, and yet he still booked a bungalow for Florence Trout.

All Jocko had to do was wait. Elliot arrived in his little town car, a black Mercedes, parked it in the same lot where Jocko had met his fate in the form of a mysterious assassin. Elliot whistled on his walk to Florence's bungalow in a Hawaiian shirt. He stayed an hour, returned to the Mercedes, and met his own mysterious stranger. Jocko crept behind him, dug the handle of a borrowed knife into Elliot's scalp. The banker's eyes disappeared into his skull. "Don't kill me, please. I'll give you anything you want."

Jocko twisted him around in the front seat of his car. "How much did you pay the hit man, huh?"

"Jocko, please. I have to go to the toilet. I'm sick."

"Good. I'm glad. You stole money from me, didn't you? And you also helped yourself to my dad's account."

"It was a crisis," Elliot said. "We'd overextended ourselves. We were short in two or three positions."

"So you took from me, covered yourself with my account."

"Jocko, I swear on my children's lives. You aren't missing a cent. It was a momentary crisis. I put back whatever I borrowed, with all the interest that was due."

"Ah, you're a sweetheart. But how did you hook up with Lothar Schill and his dancing ladies?"

"We had some German money floating around, hard cash. We knew how strong Lothar was in Cologne, and we invested the D marks in one of his nightclubs, Der Papagei."

"Nightclubs, eh? It's a smuggler's paradise. Like the Elephant's Hide. Is that where you met Florence Trout? She was one more girl with a parrot on her shoulder. And you used your fucking power of attorney to buy that club for the King of Cologne. Was it Lothar who found the hit man?"

"There was no hit man . . . it was an accident, some crazy addict."

"Yeah, an accident at high noon, next to Duck Soup . . . you'd better take my dad's money out of the Elephant's Hide. I don't like him owning a club he's never even been to."

"Jocko, I can't control the King. He's like a greedy animal."

"Then hire somebody to put him in a cage."

He should have run back to washington Square, huddled with Robevitch, and plotted Lothar's doom. But he couldn't seem to abandon the Chateau. He loitered in Duck Soup, looked at all the magazines, had lunch and dinner at The Source, and sat near the pool.

It calmed him to live at the Chateau Marmont. He could look out at the lights of Hollywood from his room. It reminded him of some enchanted airstrip without an end. He smiled when he heard a knock on his door. "Come in," he said, clutching his knife.

Florence Trout entered without her bathing cap. She still had the nervous tic near her mouth, but she was almost beautiful in a green dress.

He wanted to kiss her and then crush her head. He was startled by his own thirst for blood. He was a greedy animal, like the King.

"Florence, will Lothar come while we're making love?"

"We're not making love, Mr. Robinson . . . I once worked for Lothar, but not anymore. Katinka asked me to tell you something. She said you shouldn't return to New York."

Florence Trout left Jocko standing there with the knife in his hand, and he felt cheated. He wanted to learn her code name among the parrot girls. Tarantula? Whiplash? Carbon Monoxide?

He got on a plane to New York.

20

He wouldn't take Robevitch's advice. The little detective wanted to summon his pals from the NYPD to shut down the Elephant's Hide and separate the King from his cauliflower men. "I'll plan the attack. It will be my mission."

"No. I'll talk to the King. On my own."

Robevitch clutched his own head. "That's suicide, my son."

But Jocko walked to SoHo, went into the Elephant's Hide. The club was dark. There were no dancing ladies, no Johns to be milked, no financiers from Milan to fall in love with Katinka. Jocko had come into a cave without the slightest breeze. Then a light was snapped on, and he saw two of the King's accomplices at the bar, muscle-bound idiots, cauliflower men. They were sipping white wine that the King must have imported from Der Papagei. They winked at Jocko.

"Herr Lamplighter, the King is expecting you."

They led Jocko into an office behind the bar with dazzling white walls. The King sat behind a white marble desk that wasn't even encumbered with a telephone. Jocko could see his own face reflected in the marble.

"I'll expect you out of here by tomorrow," Jocko said. "You and your Hurricane Girls."

Lothar laughed at him. He was wearing a white turtleneck and a bloodred blazer. "The club is nothing without my demoiselles."

"Fuck your demoiselles. My dad's the owner of this clip joint, not you."

"But what if something happened to him, Herr Lamplighter? What if he should fall, or have a peculiar heart attack?"

Jocko reached across the desk to grab at Lothar, who slapped at him like a bothersome bee until the cauliflower men carried Jocko out on his ass.

He met with Robevitch. "Your pals on the NYPD, can they perform a real surgical strike?"

"Sonny, they're the best, trained in damage control."

"I don't want the King's ladies to get hurt. Not one of them. How much will it cost me to shut the Elephant's Hide?"

"You shouldn't mention money to a cop. We're a brotherhood. Certain favors have been owed to me. I had a very long career . . . but we might have to get rough with the King."

"How rough?"

"I told you. We're damage-control artists . . . we'll do what's necessary. No flourishes. Just enough juice to chase him out of Manhattan."

Jocko didn't have much pity for this King who'd taken a fourteen-year-old girl into his bed. How many other girls had he stolen from their dads? A King who pimped for love instead of money. That's what bothered Jocko the most. Katinka might have fallen for that son of a bitch, could still be crazy about the King.

"Sonny," Robevitch said, "there's no turning back once you give the green light."

Then Jocko panicked, rushed to the Elephant's Hide. The cabaret had been torn to pieces. The mirror over the bar was cracked. He couldn't find any cauliflower men sipping white wine. He had to step over a mountain of glass to get into Lothar's office. The King was tied to a chair. Both his eyes were shut. His turtleneck lay in strips around his shoulders. His nostrils were caked with blood. Jocko called an ambulance.

21

They were standing outside the building with knitted caps in their hands. They looked like naughty children. They had bandages on their faces, the King's cauliflower men. Jocko was puzzled. Did they mean to harm him and his dad in the middle of Washington Square? He didn't even ask Robevitch to shoo them away. Jocko visited with the cauliflower men, who began to cry, and blew their noses into enormous handkerchiefs.

"Herr Lamplighter, the King is dying to meet with you."

It was Jocko who rode with the King to St. Vincent's Hospital, signed him in, guaranteed to pay his medical bills. None of the doctors questioned Jocko. He was like some angel of mercy who happened to appear at the right moment.

He returned to St. Vincent's, sat with the King in a private room that looked out upon the obelisks of Wall Street. The King's arms and legs were in thick casts. Half his head was taped. He couldn't eat solid food. He had to take his nourishment with a straw.

"Herr Lamplighter," he said with a narrow smile. "You should have told me that you were mobbed up. I thought I had the right connections, but the mob was behind you."

"Those weren't gangsters, Herr Lothar. They were cops."

"Then I congratulate you. You're the King of New York . . . but what shall we do about the cabaret? All my family will be out of work."

"I'll weep for them, Lothar. Why did you steal Katinka from her dad? She was fourteen."

"Mensch, her loving father was my partner. Sergeant Baer. He was sleeping with his daughter."

"Shut up," Jocko said.

"At least she was a little happier with me."

"I'll call in the cops. They'll finish the job."

"But it won't solve the problem, Herr Lamplighter. What can we do with the cabaret?"

Jocko didn't want to leave the parrot girls stranded, with nothing to eat. He went to Robevitch. "John, how much will it cost me to fix up the Elephant's Hide?"

"What?"

"To undo the damage. Can I hire your pals at the NYPD?"

"The same lads? No. I'll have to talk to one of the carpenter teams. But I think you're crazy."

"Crazy or not, I'd like to run the Elephant's Hide.

For a little while. Dad owns the cabaret, doesn't he? Why should we watch it sit and rot?"

Robevitch wouldn't argue. He disappeared for five days, left old man Robinson in Jocko's hands. Then he invited Jocko down to the cabaret.

There were no more mountains of glass. All the rubble had been removed. The mirror behind the bar shone like a beautiful silent night. He tiptoed into the King's office, wondering what he would find. The walls were still a dazzling white. He sat behind the King's desk, stared at the reflection of his face in the merciless white marble. He was frightened. He had no idea what to do. He'd run a television show, bossed writers, producers, and technicians around. He could sit and watch the daily rushes, spin a narrative line out of complete chaos. But he didn't understand the chaos of a cabaret.

He could hear a telephone ring. The bell could have been at the bottom of the ocean. He searched the King's drawers, discovered a tiny phone.

"Hello," he said.

"Boss, is that you? What about the Schenley and the Schlitz? I'm sitting on fifty cases. Do we dump, or do we deliver?"

"Deliver," Jocko said and hung up the phone.

22

People began showing up at the cabaret, clients and employees. Suddenly a bartender appeared, then a bouncer, then the girls, who looked at Jocko with a certain wonder and curiosity in their eyes. They kissed him on the mouth, slid past his knee, like sexy snakes. Even Alfonso Walsh arrived, and Jocko wanted to kick his brains in, but he welcomed him back. He couldn't split the family.

Soon the cabaret was crowded every night. Jocko sat in his office in a silk jacket and satin shirt, lord of his own imagination. The cauliflower men would knock on his door, bearing packets of money that Jocko would stuff into his pants. He paid all his bills with cash, and when he had to, he would dip into his own accounts. He never asked questions. He lent the Elephant's Hide a liquidity it had never had.

Wise guys danced at the club, paid for every drink, begged Jocko to sit at their table. Politicians began to frequent the Elephant's Hide, with deputy police commissioners. Jocko drank champagne with them. He seemed to exist under the protection of a golden cloak. He hired musicians, fired a cashier who was taking from the till. He punched a man who had been pawing the girls, spilling whiskey into their laps . . .

He heard a strange sound. His barman was bawling, crying like a wounded bird.

"What's the matter with you?" Jocko growled. "Customers will notice . . . you'll ruin the ambience of my club."

"I can't help it," the barman said. "Please fire me. I'm no damn good."

Jocko relented a little. The barman didn't even have enough cheek to defend himself.

"What's your name?"

"Karl Sunshine."

"And who hired you?"

"Carelli."

"I don't know any Carellis. And how could he hire you? This is my club."

"Mr. Robinson, Carelli owns everything, even you. First it was Detroit. Then he wasn't satisfied. He followed me to Nice . . . and Menton."

"You were in Menton?"

"At the Princesse de Galles."

"I didn't notice you . . . not once."

"I'm with the parrot girls. I'm their catcher. I pack, I unpack. It comes to the same thing."

"How did you get involved with them? Through this Carelli?"

"No," Sunshine said. "It was Inertia. I saw her at a fashion show. It was love at first sight . . . I had a shoe company, one of the biggest in Detroit, and the parrot girls cleaned me out."

"Is that why you're sobbing?"

"It's not that. I miss Inertia."

"Sunshine, did she ever seduce you?"

"Inertia? She never had the chance."

"Is she with Carelli?"

"I doubt it. She always disappears."

Jocko grabbed Sunshine's hand. "Calm down. We'll have a drink together. And if Carelli comes in, point him out. I'd like to meet the man who owns me."

"Mr. Robinson, he's right here."

"Carelli's in my club?"

"Almost every night."

"And I'm the last to learn?"

"He doesn't like to stick out. He can't make a spectacle of himself. Manhattan isn't his native ground. He could start a civil war . . . he's sitting by the window. In a yellow coat."

Jocko couldn't see very far in the club's dim blue light. But he approached the window, found a man who wasn't much older than himself, and didn't have the manner of a thug.

"Maestro," the man said. "I'm Carelli, and I'd like to shake your hand."

"My barman says you own me."

"The barman is an ass. I ought to know. I imported him from Detroit. He was much smarter when he was making and selling shoes."

"You shoved Katinka at him."

"Never. She's my godchild. I was with her dad in Bonn and Berlin. A young soldier."

"Did you sleep with her, Mr. Carelli?"

"Jocko, why insult me? I'm your biggest fan. I bring tapes of *Lamplighter* wherever I go. It's an education. How did you get such a grip on criminals and cops?"

"I have a perilous imagination," Jocko said.

"I'd hire you as my consultant if you weren't so rich . . . did Sunshine tell you? I was a virtuoso on the violin. But I lost my luck to the German measles. It made me deaf in one ear. So God help me, I turned to crime. I'm just a figment of your perilous imagination."

Two of the local wise guys came up to Jocko.

"Mr. Robinson, it's not our business, but this guy has the plague. He's a shitbird from Detroit. We humor him, pretend he isn't around, but he shouldn't monopolize your time. Come sit with us. We'll give him three seconds to go."

Jocko had a terrible sense of déjà vu, as if he were a show runner again, condemned to writing and rewriting *Lamplighter*. Carelli wasn't wrong. Perhaps Jocko had invented him, and both of them were stuck inside a scene at the Elephant's Hide.

Carelli stood up from the table without the least bit of menace. The wise guys started to laugh. Carelli twisted around on his heels, butted the first wise guy and bit the second on the nose; blood spurted on his yellow coat, left a mysterious stain, like a child's signature, while the wise guys howled.

"Jocko," Carelli whispered, "I didn't want to break the peace. But I can't bear insults."

And he floated out of the Elephant's Hide.

The barman had already called an ambulance . . .

23

He knew it would come to this. That he would be confronted by a particular ghost, who haunted his life since the early days of *Lamplighter.* He'd wanted to forget. He'd come out of a coma and wandered the earth, following Katinka Baer. And now he was the boss of a cabaret, a bootlegger without bathtub gin. Everybody seemed to adore his gangster connections. It was part of the myth. His spare white office, his silk and satin clothes, a harem of exotic girls with parrots on their shoulder. It was glorious until the ghost arrived.

"Byron, Byron," Jocko's customers began to squeal.

It was Waldie Reynolds, the bumbling comic Jocko had found sleeping on the lot and transformed into Byron Little. The network had wanted Sean Penn, but Penn wouldn't even consider the part.

"I'd rather go with a comic," Jocko said. "I prefer an unfamiliar face."

The network griped but went along, and Byron

Little was born. He was a monster by midseason. He had problems with cocaine. He beat up a carpenter on the set, dumped his wife, ran after every woman in the crew. But he was recognized around the world after *Lamplighter*'s second year. He sang Christmas carols at the White House, was a regular on Oprah and Letterman and Larry King. *Time* called him the phenomenon of the decade, the whirlwind out of Hollywood who didn't need a film deal, his persona on the tube was so intact. Rhett Butler was an obscure gambler compared to Byron Little. Bogart and Rick's Café were relics from a slightly sweeter past. Rick couldn't have faced criminals and cops in the chaotic Humpty-Dumpty land that Byron Little had to inhabit. The tobacco industry was scared to death of Waldie Reynolds. What if he wagged his finger on prime time and told teenagers not to smoke? He could make or break a product with the blink of an eye. And he'd entered the Elephant's Hide wearing one of Byron Little's llama coats.

People mobbed him, stroked the llama skin. He signed menus and slips of paper, joked with a wise guy's wife. It took him twenty minutes to reach Jocko at the bar.

"What's the matter with your barman? He's shaking."

"Don't mind Karl. He's from Cleveland. That's where you have your biggest fans. I read it in an article."

"You're always reading," Waldie said.

Karl was dazed. "Two Lamplighters," he said.

"What the hell is he talking about?"

"He's hallucinating . . . shut up, Karl."

"Yes, Mr. Robinson."

"And go to the other end of the bar. I'm sick of you."

"Yes, Mr. Robinson."

Karl scattered, and Waldie Reynolds hugged Jocko in plain sight of the Elephant's Hide.

"Skip, we missed you. I'm mouthing lines that make me puke."

"Rewrite them, Waldie. Christ, you're the show."

Byron Little wiped his eyes. "I'm so ashamed. I didn't even visit you in the hospital."

"Waldie, did you come all the way from Malibu to hug me and catch a glimpse of the Elephant's Hide?"

"No," said Byron Little. "There's a looker."

"What looker?"

"Fabulous, I hear. A curvy Kate Moss. And she operates out of your dump with a tattoo on her shoulder. She drives men insane. I'm in the mood."

Jocko had to watch himself in the mirror. If his mask wasn't perfect, Waldie would have ripped at him.

"Ah," he said, "that little ticket."

"Jocko, what's her name?"

"Inertia."

"Come on. That's not a name. It's like a signal out of *Lamplighter*."

"But that's the signal she likes to wear . . . she's involved with thugs, Waldie. She's bad news."

Byron Little's chin began to palpitate. "If she belongs to the club, I'll buy her from you."

"She's a nomad, hops from place to place. Doesn't even have an address, except for the Elephant's Hide . . . I'll leave her a note."

The wise guys swept around Byron Little, carried him to their table. Jocko didn't have to mask his dread. He knew that somehow, somewhere, Katinka and Waldie Reynolds would meet, and she'd fall in love with that idiotic face.

His dad visited the club in his pajamas, saw the wise guys and the parrot girls, saw his own son dressed in silk, and started to cry. "My poor, poor boy. You should have stayed in California with your tofu sandwiches. You look like a thug who drifted off the lot of your television show."

But Jocko wouldn't give up the satin and the silk. He drove across the Hudson with the King's cauliflower men, who worked for him now, and borrowed Matthew Pine from that fancy prison on the Palisades. He had to rehearse Mat, reassure him. "You'll do fine. You'll have a salary and a couple of points."

"But they'll laugh at me, Jocko. You know what they'll say. The caca man is back."

"No one will laugh."

He flew out to L.A. with Mat, met with all the ogres at ABC, who didn't dare smirk in front of Jocko. Even their master, Perry Bowles, was quite meek.

"Jocko, do we have a name for the show?"

"Hurricane Ladies."

"But won't that louse up our demographics?" said one of the ogres. "These are supposed to be delicious girls."

Perry Bowles snapped at him. "Robert, they are delicious. Jocko is giving us a geography lesson. If we call them 'ladies,' they'll have instant visibility and respect in all our critical markets . . . Mat, what do you think?"

Matthew Pine wiped the sweat from his lip. "Perry, I'm a player. I always listen to my team."

It was Jocko who made him memorize those two sentences, and now the ogres changed their minds about Mat: that fallen movie star was essential to *Hurricane Ladies.*

Jocko flew back with Matthew Pine, returned him to the clinic. He didn't care what his old man had to say. He got into his silk coat and went to the club. It was already packed with people. He could feel a curious electric pull, the perfumed flesh of Hurricane Ladies. One of them was dancing with a regular at the club, a rich cokehead. Her body moved outside his rhythms. The cokehead couldn't find much of a rhythm with Katinka Baer.

24

He was beginning to grasp their signs and symbols. The code names and the tattoos. That parrot wasn't a beauty measure, an enticement to the Johns. It marked them as messengers, who couldn't be messed up by wise guys in Manhattan, or bandits in Berlin. They were transporting valuables from place to place, seducing men and women who had to be seduced. They wouldn't strip for total strangers. They would wiggle on some catwalk and go to bed with a banker from Cologne, or the banker's wife. They were really blind about sex, these nomads who created their own particular fashion show. That's why several of them were always missing. But if Lothar was in St. Vincent's with broken hands and feet, who was minding his smugglers' store?

The cauliflower men wouldn't offer him a clue, and Jocko didn't press the girls. He watched and waited, like Byron Little would have done. He didn't pursue Katinka, didn't follow her out onto the dance floor.

He would have made a fool of himself in his satin and silk.

He sat in his office, behind the bare white marble slab that could have been a coffin, and Katinka came to him. She unzipped her dress, tossed it at Jocko.

He couldn't explain why this girl with the pale-green eyes was the only one on the planet who could bring him out of his coma.

"It turns me on," she said. "Lothar's in the hospital, and you're the man behind the desk. Will you bite me if I'm bad?"

"Yes."

"Will you give me anything I desire?"

"Anything. Yes."

And she climbed across the marble, made love to Jocko on his lap.

Lothar arrived out of the blue, and Jocko cursed himself for not having spent more time with him at the hospital. He hadn't even brought him flowers or a book. The King had casts on his hands that looked like boxing gloves. He would stand in front of the mirror, start to shadowbox with the white mittens, and say, "It's a miracle. I'm back in the ring."

Jocko installed another desk in the King's old office, and they would sit face to face. The King was helpless without his hands; the parrot girls and the cauliflower men would answer the phone, feed him, scratch his back. He didn't covet Katinka.

"Herr Lamplighter," he said. "I am happy for you."

"Tell me about the smuggling."

"There is nothing to tell."

"The girls disappear, carry goods, do their little dance, and then come back to the club. Whose merchandise is it, huh?"

"Everyone's, Herr Lamplighter. And no one's. That's the nature of contraband. It's universal, like pocket money."

"And Der Papagei is the center of it all, isn't it? The world headquarters of the Hurricane Ladies."

"You are wrong, Herr Lamplighter. But I am restless. I think I will go back to Cologne."

"You're not taking Katinka," Jocko said.

"Mensch, I'm not a bloodsucker. I wouldn't steal your bride."

25

King Antonio.

It was a coronation that Katinka didn't quite understand. She wasn't even sure what she was doing in this city of the Alamo, which celebrated one hundred and eighty-seven dead men, including Davy Crockett, defenders of an impossible fort, heroes who'd disappeared in 1836, crushed by a Mexican general and his four thousand troops. Santa Anna was his name, and in her dreams he had a black moustache and a scar that ran from his eyebrow to his chin.

She was staying at the Hilton, in a suite that overlooked the River Walk. Uncle Lionello and her dad had brought her here to seduce a Tex-Mex businessman, Don Philippe, who had ten bodyguards and a big ranch. He was Jocko's age, this Philippe, and the *papa grandes* of San Antone were going to crown him at some festival filled with cowgirls and floats. She knew that Philippe wouldn't survive his own coronation. He'd offended Uncle Lionello, tried to muscle him out of Detroit.

There was another festival going on, the Starving Artists Show, which pleased Katinka, because it didn't have any coronations or floats, just a couple hundred famished painters and potters who had their own little stands near the Paseo del Rio. She looked into these artists' eyes, could read her own troubled life. They could have been with her on the catwalks in Milan, drunk, out of her mind, determined to fail. She was drawn to this festival of losers, the Starving Artists Show. She wanted to buy a piece of pottery, but her dad spun her around and nearly broke her wrist.

"No sightseeing," he said.

"But can't I help a struggling artist?"

"We didn't come here for philanthropy."

And he shoved her along the riverbank. She could see the revolving restaurant on top of the Tower of the Americas, the burnt colors of La Villita, a bit of old San Antone in the downtown district.

They entered the Hilton's Palacio del Rio, with Sergeant Baer as her sheriff. She had to bathe, put on a dark blue dress.

"You don't wink. You don't come on to him," her daddy said. "You don't play the polite little whore from Pecan Street."

"Then how do I catch his attention?"

"You sit at the bar and wait. He'll notice you, because you'll be the only bitch in the room who isn't noticing him."

"Is that a compliment, daddy?"

"Shut your stinking mouth."

He twirled her like a top and sent her down to the bar, where she sat with her legs crossed. She was right above the River Walk and she watched a very fat couple crossing one of the little stone bridges. And then the future king of the San Jacinto Festival entered the bar in a brown turtleneck and a cream-colored coat, his bodyguards scouting for a *chiquita* who would come up to Don Philippe's room for a handsome price. It puzzled her. He was beautiful and rich, a Tex-Mex caballero, with a streak of white in his hair. Why would he have to pay for sex?

One of the bodyguards approached her.

"Señorita, I would like to make a little cash deal. My *comandante*, the man in the vanilla coat, would require your services for half an hour. He will give you whatever you ask."

"Sonny," she said, "do I look like a *puta* from Pecan Street?"

"Not at all. But my *comandante* is a busy man. And—"

"If he'd like to court this *chiquita,* he'll have to do it himself."

"But he never converses with strange women. It's against his principles."

"Tell him it bothers me that he's such a principled man."

The bodyguard returned to Philippe, whispered in his ear. The caballero laughed. Then he saw Katinka, and his mouth tightened a bit. The gusto had gone out of him. He looked like a little boy in communion clothes. He sent the bodyguard back to Katinka.

"My *comandante* begs your pardon. He would like to offer you an ice cream and rent a gondola, ride with you around the river."

Katinka smiled at the bodyguard. "It isn't romantic unless he asks me himself."

The bodyguard had to shuttle back and forth. Then Philippe appeared, and he had the same scar that she'd imagined on General Santa Anna.

"You can't be Kate Moss," he said. "She's drying out in a clinic. And why would she come to San Antone?"

"To meet Don Philippe, the man who'll wear a gringo crown."

"But it's an honor. Each year we have a new King Antonio."

"For one day."

"It would be a nuisance after that. What's your name?"

"Inertia."

"It doesn't fit you . . . are you here to drink my blood?"

"Yes, Don Philippe."

She started to tremble, because she hadn't expected to like this Tex-Mex *comandante*. He could have been the ghost of Santa Anna, who'd lost a leg in combat and died a pauper. She should have kept to her suite and watched a porno film. Then she might have saved Philippe. The future king took her hand. His bodyguards had already found a gondola, which was really a long pedal boat with a pointed prow. Philippe wouldn't let his bodyguards on board. He would do all the pedaling.

"Don Philippe, should we follow behind you?"

"What will the lady think of me? That I belong in a kindergarten class?"

"But it isn't correct . . . to be alone with her on the river."

"Why? Are there crocodiles?"

"Worse."

"Follow. What do I care? But if I spot you, if I catch one glimpse, I'll become a crocodile and eat you for lunch."

And he began to pedal down the river on his flat-bottomed boat. She caught a moment of alarm in his eyes, then it passed. Did he have a premonition of who she was? Uncle Lionello's adopted daughter.

"Waldie Reynolds was here last week."

"Waldie who?" she said.

"The fat man who plays Byron Little. He said he was born in San Antone. But I don't believe it. I sat next to him at the Menger grill. He had two yellowtail steaks and more gumbo than any man could eat . . . did he send you? Because I had a curious feeling that he came to San Antone on account of me, that he was looking me over, lighting lamps that had nothing to do with his hit show."

"I never met your fat man," she said.

"But you're a little too gorgeous to sit at a bar that's my canteen."

"I model," she said.

"Not in San Antone."

"Then why'd you get into the gondola?"

"Because no gangster from Detroit's gonna crowd me. I'll pedal us as far as hell if I have to. And I just can't fight your green eyes."

She was getting dizzy in that gondola. She hadn't fallen in love with Philippe, but his little courtship rites on the river moved Katinka, almost pulled off her clothes.

"Tex," she told him, "forget my green eyes and run from San Antone."

"Only if you'll come with me."

"*Stupido,* I work for the opposition. I'm . . ."

"A charmer, my own little angel of death."

She was sobbing softly . . . like an angel. The trees along the riverbank seemed to bloom in front of Katinka's eyes. She was moving along a magic garden. And then she saw Uncle Lionello hanging from one of the stone bridges.

"Duck," she said. But it was already too late. Lionello crowned Philippe with a very sharp hunk of metal. Philippe swayed once in the gondola, grabbed her hand. Blood leaked out of his ear. His eyes closed. He dropped Katinka's hand and tumbled into the river.

"Tinka," she heard her daddy call. He was on the bridge with Uncle Lionello. "Get out of that fucking boat."

But she couldn't move. The river had become her new address. She'd hide here, join the Starving Artists

Show, paint pictures of her magic garden, beguile as many tourists as she could.

Her dad jumped into the gondola. He whacked her, squeezed both her arms, pedaled to the shore.

Lionello lifted her out of the boat.

"I'll break her bones," the sergeant said.

"Later, later," said Uncle Lionello. "First we have to disappear."

26

Her arms were black and blue. She'd been gone for a week on one of her phantom voyages. She wore dark glasses at the cabaret, and Jocko couldn't get a word out of her. He'd bathe her in his private tub, his whole body shivering as he fondled her bruises.

"Do you love me?" he asked like a beggar boy. "Just a little bit?"

She laughed for the first time since she'd come back from her voyage, and she took off her dark glasses in the tub. Her left eye was swollen. There were little cuts around the edges, as if a lunatic had wanted to redesign her face.

"You can't love any man," she said. "They're all snakes."

Jocko had to defend himself. "I'm no snake." He was wearing a washcloth that behaved like a mitten.

"I forgot," she said. "You're my satin prince."

"We could go away . . . travel to Greece. I could

lend the club to Alfonso. You wouldn't have to be one of the Hurricane Ladies."

"And what would I be, Mr. Lamplighter? Your little consort. Would you parade me around on a leash?"

"Never," Jocko said, like he was trapped inside some witness box in a sinister court of law. "I wouldn't harm you. I wouldn't show you off."

"Stop worrying. I'm crazy about you," she said, "as long as you wear your satin coat."

"It's silk," Jocko had to say.

He shivered while he bathed Katinka, he shivered in his sleep. He knew that the Devil was in the neighborhood, but it wasn't easy to pinpoint the exact spot. Jocko's neighborhood had multiplied since his years at *Lamplighter*, when he lived between the Santa Monica Freeway and Muscle Beach. The Devil could be anywhere—on Wooster Street, in Cologne, Menton in the middle. Jocko cuddled Katinka, kissed her black-and-blue marks, sensed the approach of a terrific storm. It was only November, a couple of days after Halloween, when all the girls at the club had worn scary masks, but he hadn't seen a hint of snow or heard the wind howl.

And then the storm arrived, with its own particular shape. A man in a fur coat with Katinka's pale green eyes . . . and two bodyguards. They were some kind of soldiers, that much Jocko could tell, military policemen who guarded enormous depots.

The Devil had short, iron-gray hair. The parrot girls shoved out of his way, but he caught Katinka, pretended to strike her, and she hid behind Jocko, tried to mask her own body, make herself invisible.

"How's my little girl?"

Jocko saluted him. "Hello, Sergeant Baer."

The Devil sniffed around him. "Did I hear someone speak? Who the hell am I talking to?"

"Herr Lamplighter."

"Ah, the man who's been drinking up my daughter, Jocko the billionaire . . . well, you'll have to part with some of your millions. I'm not selling her cheap."

"She's not yours to sell."

The Devil pinched one of his bodyguards. "That's a laugh. I own all these girlies, and if you had half a brain, you'd realize that I own you too."

"I thought Carelli owns me."

"Leave Carelli out of this conversation. I'll give you twenty-four hours to come up with the cash. Otherwise I might get violent and beat my own daughter to death."

27

It wasn't about money. Jocko could have afforded to buy the Devil out of business, retire him for life. But he wouldn't pay Sergeant Baer not to beat her again. The Devil had slept with his own daughter, and Jocko decided to pay him with a different currency. He went to Robevitch.

"John, I'd like this fucker removed."

"Sonny, I can't involve the NYPD. You botched our last job. You delivered that King to the hospital, and he wasn't supposed to leave the club alive. We're not going to whack a soldier for you. The U.S. Army is off limits."

"But he's a thief. He steals supplies from his own depots, moves all kinds of shit around. That's why the girls are important to him. They do his smuggling."

"He's still protected. Our generals love Germany. They can make a fortune with the right supply officer. We'd look very bad if we started butchering patriots."

"And I'm supposed to let him beat her up?"

"Stall him," Robevitch said, "write him a little check. We'll think of something. You're a college man. Did you go to school with anyone who's in the State Department? Because if we could keep the prick out of Germany, he'd fall on his ass."

"Couldn't I contribute five or ten million to the Democratic National Committee?"

"No," Robevitch said. "It's much too conspicuous."

"Then I'm lost. I won't pay him. And he will beat her to death."

"Not while John Robevitch is a breathing man," said the little detective, who had to slap his hearing aid to listen to himself.

He sat in his office, waiting for Sergeant Baer. And the cabaret began to empty around him. Alfonso went on permanent sick leave. The parrot girls found some other planet. He didn't have a single dishwasher to bring him a cup of coffee. He ordered two helpings of "Buddha's Delight" from a local Chinese restaurant. He had to fortify himself against the Devil with a forest of steamed vegetables. But it wasn't the Devil who knocked on his door. It was

Katinka in her dark glasses. She hadn't gone off with the Ladies.

"Mr. Lamplighter, will you give a girl a bath?"

She stripped in front of him, stood like a naked animal, a two-legged doe, and Jocko's heart beat with his own crazy love.

He was like a debutant delivering her to his tub. He sat her down in the slightly chipped porcelain and sponged her with a white cotton glove.

"Jocko," she said, "grab all your bankbooks and go away. Pretend you never knew me . . . Lothar and my dad planted me here. I'm their little machine. They expected you to fall in love . . . some poor television mogul who'd been sleeping for six months. They tapped me to play your mermaid."

"Mermaid," Jocko muttered.

"But I'm not that cute. And they couldn't decide whether to milk you or murder you and then steal all your money. But my dad's out of his mind. He's gonna kill you for the fun of it. He knows I like you a little. And he can't bear it when I start to like a man."

She climbed out of the tub, clipped on her dark glasses. "Whatever you're thinking, don't give my dad any cash." And then she disappeared.

28

The Devil returned with his two bodyguards. They weren't in mufti this time. They wore uniforms with gold braids and ornamental buttons. The Devil himself had three rows of colored metal bars. The bodyguards had holsters strapped to their sides. The Devil winked at Jocko and shut the door behind him.

"Did somebody sneak in and give you pitiful advice?"

"A mermaid," Jocko said.

"Well, that mermaid won't be coming around again. Do you have my money, Herr Lamplighter?"

"Dad, I could lend you a couple of thousand . . . at eighteen percent."

"Who says I'm your dad?"

A doorknob turned near the Devil and a man stepped out of Jocko's toilet in his underpants and a military tunic. He had none of the Devil's filigree except for the gold stars on his shoulder. "Jocko," he said, "I can't move my bowels with all this commotion."

The Devil stood at attention and saluted him. The bodyguards were petrified.

"General Walker," the man said, "but you can call me Hiram. We're among friends. I'm at the Pentagon, with the paymaster's office. I don't want to know your names and serial numbers. You're supply boys, and you rob from your own fucking units. But you can't rob from Jocko. He went to school with my wife's baby brother, and we're devoted to him. Am I clear?"

"Yes, sir," shouted the sergeant.

"And what would happen to the soldier who harmed him?"

"That soldier, sir, would be in very deep shit."

Sergeant Baer left with his bodyguards, and the general stepped into his trousers. "Come on," he said, "we're having turkey tonight. I don't want to be late."

Jocko drove him across the Washington Bridge.

"Jocko," the general said, "what if they catch on to us? They've been around real generals."

"Mat, you did fine. You completely paralyzed them. They're still in shock. The only thing they'll recall is a general who greeted them in his underpants."

Matthew Pine ran out of the car and into the clinic in his uniform. No one even bothered to look at his military tunic.

He sat at home on New Year's Eve, played pinochle with his dad and Robevitch, who marveled how Jocko managed to stay alive without the NYPD.

And then Herr Lamplighter got on a plane to Cologne. He felt at peace when he heard the Dom. The bell seemed to roar right through his body. He stayed in his room at the hotel, wouldn't answer the telephone. And on the second night of the new year he walked past the Old Market to Der Papagei. The parrot girls were at the bar. Sergeant Baer stood alone in his uniform and never acknowledged Herr Lamplighter. Lothar came out of his office with large white mittens.

"Mensch, you can fool that dumb soldier, not the King. There are no generals in your family."

"Where's Katinka?"

"You won't even make it to the door. I'll suck out your eyeballs with a vacuum cleaner. I'll feed you to—"

"Where's Katinka?"

And then she appeared in a red dress, without her dark glasses, purple marks around her eyes. She wouldn't smile at Jocko. A local gangster started to dance with her. Jocko shoved the gangster away.

"Mensch," he said, "that's my girl."

He held Katinka in his arms, touched the parrot on her shoulder. She looked feverish.

"Didn't I warn you, Mr. Jocko? And you jump back into the vipers' nest."

"Live with me."

She laughed in Jocko's face, but it wasn't a bitter, mocking noise. It was like the Dom's mournful bell.

"Crazyhead, I've been putting out since I was ten. I'm worse than a sexual acrobat. I slept with—"

"Who'll bathe you properly, who'll sponge your back?"

She started to cry. "Don't propose," she said. "Please." And she danced with Jocko, one bruised eye beating against his shoulder like a hummingbird.

Another soldier came into the cabaret, whispered in the Devil's ear. Jocko wanted to rescue his battered princess, sneak her out of Der Papagei. But it was too late. The Devil's accomplice was guarding the cabaret's front door. And Sergeant Baer sauntered over to Jocko with a cigarette in his mouth.

"I'll take my little girl, please."

"You lost your privileges," Jocko said. "Katinka's mine."

"I think you'd better come into the back room, Herr Lamplighter."

Katinka was shivering now. She was still in Jocko's arms. "Don't go anywhere with him. He's a snake."

Baer raised his arm to slap Katinka. But Jocko deflected the blow, blocked it with his forearm.

"You'll regret that, mister," the sergeant said. "Very soon. Should I finish you right here? Makes no difference to me. You'll never walk out of Der Papagei."

"He will, dad," Katinka said. "He'll walk out with your loving daughter."

"Shut up . . . I have a special grave prepared for defectors like you."

"No graves," Jocko said. He bowed to Baer. "Sergeant, I'm at your disposal."

"My pleasure," the sergeant said, leading Jocko to a door behind the bar. But Katinka wouldn't let go.

"You're not welcome," the Devil said. "You can't come in."

She entered the back room with Jocko. It was lit with a single bulb. The room was filled with merchandise. Jocko couldn't even find a chair.

"Herr Lamplighter, you can start begging for your life."

"Sergeant, I don't know how to beg."

"That's a pity, because your millions won't save you."

He took a pistol with a long silencer from inside his military tunic. And that's when Jocko saw a green feather rise in the air. Katinka whirled around him and dug that feather deep into the sergeant's neck. The feather was as green as a parrot's coat. Baer stumbled, trying to grab Katinka's dart, pluck it out of him. He couldn't.

He dropped in front of Jocko's feet, the slaughterer in his own little slaughterhouse.

"Tinka, we have to get out of here."

But Katinka was in a trance. Her eyes were fluttering. She began to sway.

"We have to . . ."

The King had come into the room with four of his parrot girls. "Herr Lamplighter, you can't have her . . . she's safe with me."

"Safe? How many other fathers does she have to kill?"

Lothar slapped Jocko with one of his mittens. "This is Cologne. Not one of your nighttime serials."

The parrot girls fled with Katinka.

Jocko picked up the sergeant's long gun, scratched his head with the silencer.

"Ah, it makes sense, Majesty. It was Sergeant Baer who tried to blow out my brains on Sunset Boulevard, not some drug addict . . . did Katinka know about it?"

"Of course. But she hadn't met you, Herr Lamplighter. She couldn't have anticipated your charm . . . and your stupidity."

"Why didn't you grab all my money while I was in a coma?"

"Your banker advised us against it."

"Good old Elliot Weinrib. He has power of attorney. He could have picked me clean."

"And risk having you wake up? We're businessmen. Your fortune was accumulating, Herr Lamplighter. We could afford to wait."

"It was Alfonso Walsh who turned you on to me, wasn't it?"

"Walsh? He doesn't have the brains. It was Katinka."

Jocko could feel his face explode again . . . near Duck Soup.

"King, I should have left you to rot inside the Elephant's Hide."

"You couldn't. That's your nature. Jocko Robinson. Baer didn't need a gun. You've been in a coma all your life."

"She modeled for my old man, and he let her have my secrets."

"What secrets? He started blabbering about you, complaining, or we never would have known that his son was Herr Lamplighter."

"I could have you arrested."

The King smiled into his mittens. "Mensch, this is my town. If you aren't careful, we'll pin Baer's murder on you. You'll have a long, long vacation in Cologne . . . and Weinrib won't be able to help you. Get out of here and don't ever come back to Der Papagei."

Kate Moss

29

It could have been a coma. She slept that troubled sleep of the wounded and the damned. Lothar housed her above Der Papagei, near his own quarters. Baer had been mean with the girls. Baer had been a hunter of men. The King had scuffled and killed when he had to, but he'd never tried to put out Herr Lamplighter's lamp. He wasn't an assassin. His proceeds from Der Papagei were enough for him. The King preferred to enjoy himself, not track a man with a gun. He'd never beaten one of the girls. He'd slept with them, courted Katinka, took her from the sergeant, who raged, and then realized that it would have cost him money and blood to battle the King.

Lothar had trained as a boxer; it had become a kind of aesthetic for him, a savage dance, and it was through boxing that he'd become King of Cologne. But he didn't have that wish to destroy and maim another man. So he bought Der Papagei with Sergeant Baer.

And now he was nursing Katinka. But he left most of the chores to his commando, Karl Sunshine. Karl fed her while she was asleep, Karl sang to her, read her passages from the books in Katinka's library. *War and Peace. Great Expectations. The Glass Key.* Karl barely understood a word. He couldn't comprehend murder or romance on a page. His imagination was limited to Katinka . . . and a planet of shoes.

He fed her applesauce while the King watched from a distance.

"Lothar, will she ever wake up?"

"Let her dream, will you?"

"But she could fall very far . . . in her sleep."

"Not as far as her own dad. Mensch, she's still alive. And you'd better keep her that way."

30

Jocko returned to his cottage near Muscle Beach, stepped onto Ocean Front Walk, and half of Hollywood's dispossessed actors and writers besieged him for a job. He had to run and hide in his Dart. He drove to his production company, marched into his office, locked the door, and outlined an episode of *Lamplighter.* The cops take over a little town in New Jersey, fling out the mob, and rule with the help of local politicians and judges. They collect graft, sell dope, hire themselves out as contract killers. Citizens have no one to complain to, not the old mob or the new police, suddenly the fattest cats around. The town has become a twilight zone. Kids are afraid to rumble in the streets. Restaurants close their doors early. Prostitutes can only work out of registered cabarets, while the cops hang out at a bowling alley called the White Owl. There are no more criminals to catch, only whores to sleep with and cash to collect. The cops brand their women with a mark on the backside, a little blue ice pick, their own idea of law and order.

The White Owl is always full. It's much livelier than a police station.

Exiled to another part of Jersey, the mob summons Byron Little. Its chief, an Irishman named Harlequin Ed, cries in front of Byron. "Lamplighter, give us back our town. We'll pay you anything."

"Why haven't you opened shop somewhere else? One town is as good or bad as another."

"We were born there. It's our home."

Harlequin, New Jersey, population 6,009.

The Lamplighter names his price. Ed agrees. But there's one catch. Byron Little won't work without Mickey O'Dell, a mobster who turned into the town drunk. He lives in a cardboard hut at the edge of Harlequin. The cops consider him as their mascot.

The Lamplighter sneaks into Harlequin, finds Mickey O'Dell in his hut. There's a curious bond between them. Byron had put the Mick away when he was a prosecutor, sent him off to the state prison farm. But Byron Little has always been the strangest of lawmen. He wrote to the Mick. He was a kind of half-crazed Christ who believed in redemption. The Mick wrote back. The two of them became pen pals. And that's how Byron Little lost his pants as a prosecutor. He was much too chummy with the prison population. There were rumors of an indictment. He was forced to resign. His pen pals recommended him to certain parties, and Byron Little began to light lamps for the mob.

He has trouble with Harlequin's court jester, who won't come out of his cardboard hut.

"Mick," the Lamplighter says. "I need your music. You have to distract the bad boys, buy me a little time."

"I'm history if I help you, a dead man."

"We can clean out Harlequin, you and me."

"Tell that to Big Ray."

Raymond Hatch, the police chief of Harlequin, had been a baker as a boy, and Harlequin was his personal bake shop. He delivered candy and cake to the faithful, and starved the rest. He kept judges and prostitutes in his pocket, ran his own little police state from the White Owl.

"Mick, how many lamps have I lit?"

"You can't oust the Baker. He's too big."

"Come on. He's like any fat cat. He'll fold."

And like a timid mouse, Mickey joins Byron Little, walks into the White Owl. He's harmless. He can dance or bowl with Heather Just, the Big Man's lady. She's a sad-eyed gamin, the local Kate Moss, with a little blue ice pick engraved on her ass. Ray's jester is in love with her.

"Heather," he whispers. "There'll be fireworks. Pack your gear and go."

"Why? I'm mistress of the Owl."

"Not for long. Byron Little's in town."

She starts to laugh. "That ninny. He can't even light a match."

But Byron has already doused the bowling alley's bunkerlike walls with kerosine. And Raymond's headquarters starts to burn. Cops and women have to abandon their bowling balls and run for their lives. The Big Man is furious. Who would dare attack him in his sanctuary? Not Harlequin Ed. But to show his authority and his reach, he demolishes a few of Ed's boys, and settles into his original bailiwick, the police station on Tilbury and Vine. He turns it into a fortress, puts bars on every window, fireproofs the walls. But when his cops venture out of the fort, they never come back. His collectors can't collect. He has no bottled water, and his taps bleed a dark red rust.

"It can't be Harlequin Ed," he cries. "Ed doesn't have the brains to topple me."

One by one his lackeys abandon him. He's alone with Heather Just. Without water, they start choking to death. They crawl out of the police station. Harlequin Ed and his gang have already reoccupied the town.

"Who was it?" Raymond hisses. "Who was your commander in chief?"

And that's when he sees Byron Little with his own court jester. "I should have figured. The Lamplighter."

Harlequin Ed and his gang approach Raymond and Heather with hammers in their hands. But the Lamplighter is already "wounded." He can't stop gazing into the gamin's sad eyes. He steps in front of the hammers soon as Ed starts to strike.

"Byron," says Harlequin Ed with a gentle growl.

"He killed my men. He and his witch have to suffer."

"I lit lamps for you. No hammers in the head."

And Big Ray vanishes with Heather into the dust.

31

Waldie Reynolds was arrested on Rodeo Drive. A bunch of salesmen had teased him, called out from their car, "Byron Little doesn't have a dick." Waldie battled with them, broke a salesman's jaw, and now he sat in the little jailhouse behind the Hall of Justice.

Jocko found him chatting with his jailors in their canteen. He had Jocko's script stuffed in his pocket.

"Hi, Skipper. Have a Coke."

"Can't we talk in private?"

"Sure." Byron clapped his hands. "Out, out." And all the jailors fled from their own canteen. Waldie took the script out of his pocket and hurled it at Jocko.

"It stinks. Byron Little doesn't set bowling alleys on fire. I won't play a pyromaniac."

"But that's the charm of the show. Byron comes out of his cocoon."

"You're in a cocoon, mister. A permanent cocoon. You lied to me."

"Lied about what?"

"Inertia. She's a prostitute. And you wouldn't even share her . . . you want that hungry little bitch for yourself."

"She's no prostitute."

"She's worse . . . I have my spies. Katinka Baer. She romances men and ruins them."

"Then you ought to be glad I saved your hide."

Byron Little rose up from his chair and tried to clobber Jocko. The jailors returned. "It's all right," Byron said. "I was having a muscle spasm." And he chased them out of their canteen again.

"Heather Just," Byron said. "With a blue ice pick engraved on her ass. That's your magic, Jocko. You wrote Katinka Baer into the script."

Jocko looked into Byron's eyes and shivered. He saw a madness that wouldn't bend. The Devil hadn't died in Cologne . . .

"Where's that little looker, huh? That kinky spider?"

"I don't know," Jocko said.

"Find her for me, Skip. Or Byron Little doesn't set foot in Harlequin, USA."

Waldie was let out of jail. *Lamplighter*'s lawyers had settled with the salesmen, who turned sheepish about Byron Little. "We wouldn't dream of damaging the best goddamn detective in the world."

Waldie reappeared on the *Lamplighter* set, punched a producer, ate a ham sandwich, fondled one or two of the female extras, and tossed Jocko's script to the production manager.

"That's our next shoot."

"Waldie, I can't just . . ."

"It's Jocko's baby. You want to anger the boss?"

The entire production company went to work on "Harlequin, USA," while Waldie sat in his trailer. And when Jocko arrived on the first day of shooting, Byron paused in the middle of a scene. "Skipper, you're blocking my sight lines."

Jocko could have halted production, but a rift between him and Waldie would have rattled the networks. He sat in his bungalow near Muscle Beach, watching the rushes. Byron Little keeps leering at Heather.

The phone rang. It was Waldie. "You wouldn't let me have Katinka. So I'll take Heather Just. It's tit for tat."

"Byron never gets to kiss a girl. That's fundamental to the show. He's a recluse, a monk."

"Not anymore."

Waldie had a hunger he couldn't control. A hunger to tear, to damage beyond redemption. He had his own motorcycle gang, bikers who did whatever he asked. Their leader was a thug called Mitch, who looked like a moronic Viking. Mitch might kidnap a girl for Waldie, beat up a man who owed him money, or race up and down a deserted highway until some fool appeared in a pickup truck. The bikers would surround the truck, with Waldie sitting on Mitch's saddle and wearing a mask, so the fool couldn't recognize him. The bikers would drag the fool out of his truck, rip off his clothes, and Waldie would light matches on the fool's chest, play the barber, cut the fool's hair, punch him, kick him, until the fool broke down and begged for his life. The fool had to beg, or Waldie would have stabbed him with his scissors.

Pain was the only force that ignited him. The coke he snorted was never enough. It couldn't relieve the terror and the boredom of being Byron Little. He was a fat man who had to be light on his feet. He danced in front of the camera, dreaming of who else he might wreck. One of the bitches his gang had kidnapped, a certain Brenda, had gone back to her beau. Brenda was a shoe clerk in Silverlake and an artist's model. He'd brought her to the apartment tower that served as his harem. But Brenda had bolted, and he'd tracked her to a cottage near the old Charlie Chaplin studio, at Sunset and LaBrea.

He whistled while he marched behind Chaplin's row of gingerbread houses, arrived on Brenda's porch. Mitch was already there with his bikers. The cottage had once been a watchman's shack that belonged to the Chaplin compound. It was utterly isolated and had its own little garden. The bikers had sat Brenda's beau in a wicker chair and hoisted the chair above the porch with several pulleys and a long piece of rope. He was an actor, Joe Collars. Waldie had given Joe a bit part on *Lamplighter* as payment for stealing his girl.

"Boss," Mitch said, "how do you like the way we strung him up? . . . we can raise him to the roof or drop him on his head."

Waldie heard someone sob. He didn't even have to look. It was Brenda.

"Please, Mr. R., please . . . I'll be good."

She came up to Waldie, her blouse unbuttoned.

"Did you do that, Mitch? Did you touch my merchandise?"

"She was with the hillbilly boy, having a little heave-ho on their hammock."

"Well, button her up, Mitch. I don't want half the world peeking at Brenda."

"Boss, nobody's here."

"You're here, Mitch. That's enough."

The biker buttoned her blouse.

"Hiya, Joe," Waldie said, watching a pair of legs dangle above him. Waldie was jealous. Joe Collars had washboard abdominals and a woman's silky eyes.

"You can't have my gal, Mr. Reynolds."

"Didn't I hire you, Joe? We had a deal . . . Mitch, haul him down."

Mitch pulled on the rope, and the chair began to descend. Waldie took out his cigarette lighter and set Joe's pants on fire. Brenda screamed and slapped at the burning pants.

"Mr. R.," she said. "I'll be your slave."

"Not without Joe's consent."

"Burn me to blazes," Joe said.

Waldie twisted around on his heels and held the lighter close to Brenda's scalp.

"Hair burns awful fast."

Joe Collars started to cry.

"Ah, take her then."

Waldie vanished with Brenda, leaving Joe Collars strapped in the chair. His bikers followed behind him. He wasn't even interested in the bitch. He'd guard her a couple of weeks and send her back to Joe.

32

Katinka opened her eyes. She must have been on a long sea voyage. Her head was rocking and her mouth was dry. But she didn't see any portholes, not the hint of an ocean. She hadn't lost her mind. She was upstairs, above Der Papagei, in the King's own closet. And she had Catcher Karl as her chamberlain. He was standing near her, like one of the Seven Dwarfs. And she was the modern Snow White, a murderess without a mask. Kate Moss, she'd been dreaming of Kate Moss, who tossed furniture out of hotel windows during her fights with Johnny Depp. It was Kate Moss who was on an ocean liner, in the middle of a défilé. And Katinka was with her, sipping champagne at high noon, smoking grass, but Katinka couldn't fit into her dress, which was made of iron instead of silk, iron that clung to her like a claw. The iron couldn't capture Katinka's breasts. She'd never been a gamin, not even at twelve. She'd developed too early, the doctors had told her. She was on the catwalks of Milan at fifteen, but it was more like piracy than a modeling career. Some man always owned her, lent her out to other men.

"Katinka."

Her catcher was crying. "I'm so glad. You're out of your coma. I'll tell the King."

"Shhh," she said. "It's our secret. Wasn't a coma, Karl. It was a long, enchanted sleep."

"But who's the enchanter?"

"Guess."

"I can't," Karl said. "I'm crazy with happiness. Who's the—"

"Herr Lamplighter."

"Him? He's like the King. He has a cabaret."

"But he doesn't buy and sell people, Karly . . . help me out of bed."

"You're too weak."

"We can't stay here . . . in Lothar's prison."

"He's the King of Cologne. Where could we hide?"

"In our heads."

"Katinka, don't make fun of me. I'm a shoeman without a single shoe, naked as Adam and Eve. And I don't even have the advantage of a garden. Der Papagei is all we've got."

"We've got each other. Dress me, Karl."

"But the King took all your clothes."

"Then you'll have to get them."

"I'm scared," Karl said. "The King will break my bones. He's the enchanter. He talks on the telephone with Carelli."

"But you're the catcher, Karl. Catch my clothes."

And Karly slipped out of the closet, his back all bent. She wasn't on an ocean liner. She was in a rehabilitation clinic, drying out with Kate Moss. One of Katinka's own troupe, Skeleton or Nightmare, had smuggled in a bottle of champagne. And they began to drink, right under the doctor's eyes, out of a little leaky hospital slipper. Snow White.

She heard footsteps. Clop, clop, clop, like the clogs of a giant. It couldn't have been Karl, but Karl returned with a bottle of champagne and a bloody mouth. Lothar stood behind him, wearing silk pajamas and wooden shoes. Katinka watched the bottle sway in Karl's hands. Kate Moss, she muttered to herself.

"We'll celebrate," Lothar said. "You're with us again . . . should I summon the girls?"

"King, where's my clothes?"

"I dropped them in the incinerator after Karl went looking."

"He's our catcher."

"He'll catch hell," Lothar said. "He'll piss blood in Cologne."

"Why'd you burn my clothes?"

"Evidence, my love. You did your dad with one of Carelli's darts, or don't you remember? I had to destroy all your tracks . . . Katinka no longer exists. The sergeant never had a daughter. Don't worry. I'll invent another fable for you."

"I don't need your fables. I need my clothes."

He handed Katinka a glass of champagne. "Drink."

"No," Katinka said. "Not with you."

"Should I sock Karl again, my love?"

Katinka drank the champagne.

"You can't imagine how loyal I am. A man wants to buy you."

"What man?"

"Waldie Reynolds. Herr Lamplighter's other half. Money's only paper to him. He offered me a couple of million. He's crazy about you."

"Then why didn't you deliver the goods?"

"You'd only put a dart in his neck. And that dart might come flying back to Der Papagei."

Lothar finished his champagne, left the bottle on the night table, bowed to Karl. "Shoemaker, mind her for me. And no tricks."

Katinka waited until he clop-clopped down the stairs. Then she wiped the blood from Karl's mouth, rocked him in her arms, and they drank champagne together.

"Tinka, we'll never, never get out of here."

Harlequin, USA

33

He was coming out of Duck Soup, returning to his Dart, when he could feel a presence behind him, like the hot little wind that only a human could make. Not again, he groaned. *Variety* would laugh at him. "Show Runner Murdered Twice in Same Parking Lot." He turned around to face his attacker with a closed fist. But he wasn't fast enough. A hammer landed on his head . . .

He woke in a dark room. He could hear the sound of water, but it wasn't the sea. Jocko was near a swimming pool, not some surfer's paradise. A light was clicked on, and he recognized his own writing partner, Miles Farmer. Miles was too much of a coward to have kidnapped him all on his own. Jocko wanted to slap Miles, but he couldn't move very far; both his ankles were chained to the bed he was lying on. And Miles wore a gun inside his belt, like the gangsters of Harlequin.

"You're working for that madman."

"He gave me a bonus," Miles said.

"But you wanted to be a show runner. Didn't I get *Hurricane Ladies* for you? And you toss your future into the garbage can."

"No. Now I have two futures. *Lamplighter* and *Ladies*. Waldie says I can run both shows."

"You turned him on to Katinka, didn't you?"

"It's only natural. He wants what you want. I had to tell him about Tinka. I couldn't resist . . . don't tangle with him. I swear. It's suicide."

Miles Farmer left, and Jocko listened to people splash in the pool. Waldie owned apartment towers in Santa Monica, West Hollywood, and Silver Lake. Some of them he kept deserted, like the La Cienega, where he would bring the "babes" he loved to beat up. He couldn't have an erection until he kicked them and punched them and they started to scream.

A woman appeared with a tofu burger from The Source. Jocko had lost his appetite with that hammer in the head. He couldn't think of food. The woman undressed.

"It's on the house. Don't you want a freebie? I'm damn expensive, you know. I stood in line, got you a burger, and you won't even taste it . . . did a cat bite your tongue?"

A voice shot out at Jocko, seemed to scratch his back. "That's adorable, Brenda. But you're supposed to feed him lunch, not your fucking body."

It was Waldie, wearing white gloves.

"Mr. R., I—"

He kicked her like a donkey.

Jocko couldn't close his eyes and disappear into some dream. "Waldie, will you stop that?"

"Shut up," Waldie said while he kicked and kicked. "You're nothing. You don't exist." But his anger died suddenly. He stroked Brenda and put hundred-dollar bills on her chest. "Papa's sorry. Papa didn't mean any harm."

He walked her out of the room, kissed her forehead, and returned to Jocko with a handkerchief in his eyes. Byron Little was sobbing like a baby. He edged close to Jocko, whose hands were still free, and Jocko wanted to rip his nose off. But Byron recovered from his crying fit and tapped Jocko gently with a finger of his glove.

"I was a fat man sleeping on the studio lot until you found me. You should have left Waldie alone. It's no picnic being Byron Little. I have all these crazy fans. I have to talk out of the side of my face, with your fucking words. I want my old self back."

"Then quit the show."

"Stupid, I'm Byron Little. Your cash cow."

"And what will you do, Waldie? Keep me here?"

"Why not? You have all the amenities. Babes. Terrific grub. And if you're a good boy, I'll let you have twenty minutes down at the pool. Just write me scripts about Harlequin, or I'll make you suffer longer and harder than you've ever suffered before."

"It's the end game, isn't it, Waldie?"

"What end game? You're talking like Byron Little. And that's my privilege."

"Now that you have me, you can't afford to let me go . . . it's a little dance of death."

"Not if you cooperate."

Jocko had to laugh. "You'll kill me anyway . . . you've been waiting for me to die since *Lamplighter* began."

"You took my soul, Skipper. That wasn't nice. But I need your magic hand."

"Ask Miles."

"Miles can't write shit. Do yourself a favor. Give me more Harlequins, and I might not break your hump."

"No."

"Then we'll have a little foreplay. I don't have time to get serious."

Waldie took off his belt slowly, like a male striptease, whacked Jocko on the ear with the buckle, then he knelt down, grabbed Jocko's chains, tugged on them until Jocko fell off the bed. "Having fun?" He straddled Jocko, whipped him with the long hard tongue of the belt, then socked him with the glove, until Jocko was dizzy with despair. He couldn't counter Waldie's syncopations.

"Are you ready to write?"

"No."

Waldie began the process again until Jocko blacked out.

He woke with Brenda beside him. She was sobbing and washing his face.

"Lamplighter, he'll murder me if you don't write."

"Brenda, I wish, I wish . . ." And Jocko blacked out again.

He wasn't sure how many times he was beaten, or if Waldie himself had administered the blows. He could only see out of one eye, and even that eye was blurred. "Brenda," he asked in the dark, "are you still alive?"

But she wouldn't answer him. And suddenly he started to dream. Whole stories popped into his head, as if the beatings had spurred his imagination. He was trapped within Harlequin's little tornado of crime. Heather Just was speaking to him, purring. She must have been naked. He recognized the blue ice pick engraved on her ass. "Lamplighter," she said, "can you ever love me?"

He was the one who was crying now.

34

Harlequin provided Jocko with a rocking rhythm, like a lullaby he didn't want to wake out of. Brenda put a salve on his back, and the marks from Waldie's belt went away. He'd swim in the pool around midnight. He thought of his mother, dying day by day in his father's house, while the old man kept mistresses on another floor. Jocko had gone to California as soon as he could, but he'd abandoned his mom, left her with her bottles of whiskey. She was the one who guarded Jocko from Mr. Robinson's wrath, took him to museums with a bottle in her handbag. Whatever brutality had surfaced in *Lamplighter* was the brutality of a son who couldn't protect his mother, who had to watch her weaken.

Waldie arrived in a rage. "Where's my scripts?"

He beat up Brenda, shaved all her hair, forced her to lie down in front of Jocko like a bald wraith. Then he put on his white glove and went to work . . .

"Herr Lamplighter."

Jocko opened one eye. The King of Cologne was standing near him, Lothar Schill, with all his parrot girls. They'd covered Brenda with a blanket and were painting her skull with watercolors. Waldie's secret penthouse at La Cienega had been converted into some kind of headquarters. It was busy as a cabaret. Jocko sat with his chains and watched the incredible buzz around him.

"Mensch, are you awake or not?"

"Where's Inertia?"

"With Herr Reynolds, naturally. I sold Tinka to him. He looked at her once and lost the urge to beat your brains in. That's what she does to men. You ought to know, Herr Lamplighter. But we have to mend you a little."

"Don't come near me, King."

"Girls," Lothar said. Skeleton, Sloth, and Nightmare stripped Jocko, scrubbed his body with eucalyptus soap, and went back to their watercolors and Brenda's skull. Jocko recognized the shoeman, Karl Sunshine, and Carelli, that gangster from Detroit. They were with Elliot Weinrib and Florence Trout. "Christ, the whole congregation is here . . . Elliot, am I a pauper yet?"

But Katinka arrived with Waldie before Elliot could answer. She was laughing into the Devil's eyes. And she wouldn't glance at a miserable rat in chains.

"Show runner," Waldie said, fondling Katinka, "aren't we a great couple? Who needs Heather Just?"

Carelli coughed. He was wearing a *Lamplighter* crew jacket and a *Lamplighter* cap.

"Skipper, we're in the woods without you."

"I don't get it. You own half of Detroit."

"I bought into your production company. I'm on the set every day. We can't survive without your scripts."

Florence Trout removed a golden pin from a fat dossier. And Jocko's melancholy deepened by the minute. He felt like a spectator in some gangsterland he'd spun out of his own head.

35

I'm bigger than God. Fatter, richer . . . and all I want is you."

Katinka smiled at Waldie, pretended . . . she didn't have to pretend. She could romance a crocodile if she had to.

She'd wiggled her ass out of Cologne, convinced Lothar that what he needed was a new Papagei, next to Farmers Market and the kosher delis on Fairfax, where movie stars could dance with Lothar's parrot girls.

"I'll sacrifice myself," she'd told the King. "Sell me to the fat man. He'll buy you a club."

"And what will you get out of it?"

"Fun," she said. "I'm frivolous."

"You're in love with Herr Lamplighter, aren't you?"

She'd have spoiled her own grift if he caught her in a lie, and he'd have kept her in Cologne.

"I have an itch for him. It's incurable."

"And what about the fat man?"

"I'll manage him too."

And now they were in the fat man's domain. With Carelli, who seemed to own a piece of everyone and everything, who gobbled up whatever there was to gobble, who demanded nothing and collected what he could. Carelli. If you looked at him a little too long, he'd bite your nose off . . .

They were in a stretch limousine, a gigantic blue caterpillar with wheels. Skeleton, Nightmare, Sloth, Lazybones, and Inertia, with the fat man, Lothar, and Uncle Lionello, drinking champagne. The fat man was already out of his skull. His eyes were fluttering.

"Lionello, I want to marry your niece."

"You can marry her without my permission. She's not a child. And she's not really my niece. I knew her father."

"Where the hell is the old man?"

"We don't like to talk about him," Carelli said. "Tinka planted a dart in his neck. They didn't get along."

"That's my kind of girl," the fat man said. "She's unpredictable, right, babe?"

Katinka smiled at the fat man. He was fondling her breast. His hand felt like a claw.

"Elliot," he shouted, "where the fuck are you?"

Elliot Weinrib was sitting in another piece of the caterpillar with Florence Trout.

"Elliot, will you draw up a contract? Mr. Schill gets his club. What should we call it? Elephant's Hide West? And I get Katinka."

"I'll have to confer with my legal department," Elliot said.

"Your legal department is sitting in your lap . . . Florence does all the dirty work. And Mr. Carelli gets his usual twenty percent, under the table." The fat man winked into his champagne. "Lionello, what do you do with all the cash?"

"Shhh, Herr Reynolds," Lothar said. "You shouldn't ask a man to give his secrets away . . . and Herr Lamplighter, what if people come looking for him?"

"Let 'em look. That kid's always in a coma. And when he's useless to us, we'll—"

"Lend him to the boys at Muscle Beach," Katinka said.

Uncle Lionello was staring at her. And she had to waltz the fat man in another direction or Lionello would see right under her black dress, into the ravages of her heart, where she lived with Jocko in some haunted house and watched his wounds go away . . .

"We never talked about my contract," she said.

"What contract, babe? You have Waldie. That's enough."

"Uncle Lionello might not agree. Uncle looks after my interests."

"Katinka's right," Carelli said. "Not a written contract. Verbal will do. We're all witnesses."

"Babe," the fat man said, "what do you want?"

"My catcher, Karl. You'll have to employ him."

"At Elephant's Hide West?"

"I don't care. But he has to have a health plan . . . the same with all the girls."

"Jesus, am I marrying one model, or a whole platoon?"

"A platoon," Katinka said, while Waldie touched her nipple, and she wanted to send him hurtling out of the limousine, into some forgotten canyon where he'd never be found. But the limo stopped and they all piled out and entered a club on Wilshire Boulevard that looked like a broken pillbox. It was called the Sick Squire, and it was the fat man's favorite haunt. People grabbed at him, had to touch the television hero. They started touching Katinka too. "Kate Moss," they shouted, "Kate Moss." She couldn't control the hysteria in their eyes, the enormity of their wish.

So she was Kate Moss at the Sick Squire. Customers offered her champagne and free coke. The fat man wouldn't let go of her nipple. Lothar must have seen the malice behind her idiotic grin. He pulled her away from the fat man and his admirers and propelled her out onto the dance floor. Katinka could barely breathe. The suck of air conditioning, mixed with perfume and sweat, made her dizzy.

She would have swooned if Lothar hadn't held her in his arms. "You can't kill him."

"Why not?"

"Because he's Lionello's partner. I'll have my own club."

"Congratulations."

A biker appeared, took over the Sick Squire. Mitch.

He had strands of tobacco in his moustache. His gang was behind him. He grabbed Katinka away from the King.

"Kate Moss," he said, "this dance is mine."

She wanted to sock him, but he held her wrists.

"Uncle Lionello," she screamed.

Lionello was already there. "Little boy, the lady doesn't like you."

"Who's a little boy?"

The fat man arrived, pulled on Mitch's moustache. The biker started to blink. "Sorry, boss. I didn't know that Kate is your people."

"She's my fiancée."

He took Katinka in his arms, while the bikers fled.

"I'll dance with you, babe. You'll never feel lonely."

36

It was 4:00 A.M. when they returned to the tower. The fat man was half asleep. Katinka let him find his own boudoir. She shared a mattress with Nightmare and Lazybones. Lothar and Lionello had already gone off to their suite at the Hollywood Roosevelt Hotel. They shunned Beverly Hills, preferred the sadness of Hollywood. Katinka had some of the same sadness. She'd been reading about Rita Hayworth—Margaret Carmen Cansino of the Dancing Cansinos before she was a movie star. Margaret had started dancing with her dad in Tijuana when she was twelve. Eduardo Cansino. She pretended to be Eduardo's wife. Eduardo plucked her out of school, taught her to sexually provoke all the customers in any nightclub or casino where they danced . . . and took her into his bed, like Katinka's dad had done. The Good Sergeant Baer, who let her "model" for other men. No wonder she'd become an acrobat, and a little ice goddess.

The goddess got out of bed. She marched across the plains of Waldie's penthouse in her pajama tops. She bumped into Karl. Her catcher was drinking coffee in the kitchen. His hands were trembling.

"I don't like it here."

"Karly, we won't be staying long, I promise. Didn't I get you out of Cologne?"

"But the King's a saint compared to the fat man. His bikers have a blowtorch. They could set our hearts on fire."

She kissed her catcher and continued to cross the plains. She stopped at the Lamplighter's bed. Brenda, his bald nurse, slept on a mattress beside him, but the Lamplighter was awake.

She stooped near Jocko in her pajama tops, touched the marks on his face. "Lamplighter, did you miss me?"

"Every goddamn minute of my life . . . but the King sold you to Waldie. You're his concubine."

"His bride," Katinka said. "I wormed a contract out of him. But I'm used to husbands. I married my father when I was twelve . . . aren't you going to ask me for a cuddle and a kiss? I've never made love with a prisoner of war."

She saw the shiver in his eyes. She rocked him in her arms, sat with him until he fell asleep, returned to her bed, and started to dream about Katinka of the Dancing Baers. Her father would drive her to a little hotel on the Rhine, next to the house where Beethoven was born, and she'd dance for strangers. They were soldiers and high-ranking civilians, the burghers of Bonn, and she had to play Lolita for them. Sometimes a captain or a general would grow infatuated with Baer's little girl, pretend to be her father, take her to lunch and lectures at the university and visits to Beethoven's house. He'd fondle her on Beethoven's narrow bed, hum half a symphony, give her a bundle of cash.

"I ought to nail your father to the wall. But I wouldn't have met you without him, child."

"I'm not a child, general."

"Then what are you?"

"The love of your life."

And he'd laugh, this general in civilian clothes, with a steel hand he'd inherited from Vietnam.

Her dad wouldn't give her a dime.

"Did you say rotten things about me to the general?"

"No, daddy. I told him we were a team. The Dancing Baers."

He'd hit her and take off her clothes. He couldn't hum Beethoven or stroke her with a steel hand . . .

She woke with a pounding in her ears, a maniacal laugh. It was the fat man. She ran toward his laughter.

He was whipping Jocko with his belt and shoving Nightmare and Skeleton away. "Where's my scripts?"

Lothar and Lionello were with him, and Miles Farmer, who was playing with a gun, tossing it in the air like a hot potato, while the fat man whipped, and Jocko's face grew bloody.

"Waldie," Lionello said, "that's enough."

"Uncle, this isn't Detroit. What will you do? Bite off my ear? They'll have to shut down *Lamplighter*, and you'll lose a fortune."

Lothar remained silent. He didn't want to contradict Waldie, or he'd have to run home without his new club.

It was up to the sergeant's little girl. Lionello wouldn't even look into her eyes.

"Waldie dear," she said. The fat man turned, recognized Katinka in her pajama tops.

"Be with you in a minute, babe. Haven't had my morning exercise."

"Neither have I . . . come."

The fat man grinned. Then he winked at Miles, who followed him and Katinka to her mattress, stood on guard, while the fat man dropped his pants, whistled "Tea for Two," snorted coke from a silver spoon around his neck, and sank into the mattress. Katinka mounted him like a wildcat. "Incredible girl," he said. Katinka tore the silver spoon from its little chain and dug it into the fat man's throat, under his Adam's apple. His legs quivered and then stopped, quivered and stopped.

Miles dropped the gun and ran. "I can't get involved . . . I'm a show runner. I'll lose my show."

Lothar and Lionello arrived with the parrot girls and Karl. But she was still dreaming of Beethoven and the Dancing Baers. No one had ever touched her like the general had touched her with his steel hand. He could hypnotize a twelve-year-old girl. She would have danced for him the rest of her natural life. But she didn't have a natural life.

"Kitten," Lionello said, "give me the gun."

She shot him in the heart.

Lothar looked at Lionello.

"King," she said, "say your prayers."

The King appealed to Nightmare and Lazybones. "Children, talk to her . . . the strain has been too much. Tell her that we're on her side."

"King, tell me yourself . . . didn't we live together? Wasn't I your perfect pet?"

"I took you out of your father's house."

"And made a profit from my bones."

"But you modeled . . . I brought you to Milan."

"And abandoned me to your gangster friends. I was fifteen . . . and stayed fifteen."

She shot him twice. Blood spilled from his mouth and he fell on top of Lionello.

"Karl," she said, "don't be scared. I'm not crazy."

She returned to Jocko, lay down beside him, and fell into a long, enchanted sleep.

The Princess of Echo Park

37

She spent one night in jail. Police surgeons examined Katinka, consulted with a judge and the court psychiatrist, and shipped her to the county asylum near the Hollywood Freeway and Echo Park. She was given a white sheet to wear, had to sit in a huge tub that hissed boiling water at her. They called it hydrotherapy. Her skin was all red from the burning water. And she didn't have much peace at the asylum. Her picture was spread across the *L.A. Times,* together with the fat man. "DERANGED MODEL MURDERS BYRON LITTLE AND TWO GANGSTERS IN NORTH HOLLYWOOD SINK." Katinka's face was on all the television screens. She'd become a celebrity, the princess of Echo Park. Nurses, patients, and guards demanded Katinka's autograph. She had to keep signing her name.

A madwoman with a terrible tic approached her in a blue hospital gown. Suddenly the tic disappeared. "I'm a syndicated columnist, Harriet Hall. I'd like an exclusive. Do you realize how hard it was to sneak in here? I can get you a book contract. Three mil. You don't have to scribble a word. I'm a ghostwriter, and I'm great at it. Did Byron Little torture you?"

"I don't remember Byron," she said.

"You totaled him. How could you forget?"

All she could remember was the Dancing Baers. How she hated her father, and wanted to please him. How she learned to dance, in and out of bed. How she wasn't really made for modeling in Milan . . .

The hospital had its own garden, and the nurses would accompany Katinka on long hikes, while people gathered outside the gates to spy on the princess and photograph her when they could. "Inertia, pose for us, please."

And she'd rush back into the asylum.

Her bed was as narrow as Beethoven's. She was in a dormitory with women who watched themselves in the mirror night and day, tore at their own hair, gave birth to a million babies, talked to Marilyn Monroe in their sleep. It was one more hurricane in a life of hurricanes . . .

An ambulance drove Jocko to Misericordia. It was like a homecoming ball. The sisters took his temperature and fed him bagels from Farmers Market. He tried to call Katinka and couldn't get through. He sent her catcher, but the asylum wouldn't let Karl through the gates. She was under some kind of insidious house arrest.

County prosecutors stalked Jocko's bed. They looked at his temperature chart and didn't say a word. Then their chief arrived, "Lucky Lucifer" Brown.

"What are you doing with Katinka?"

"Warehousing her," said Lucky Brown. "I'm building my case. But you're our weakest link. You'll get on the stand and defend that little witch. And the jury just might believe you . . . she's a killer, Mr. Robinson. And I might even name you as her accomplice. Unless you agree to cooperate."

"You'd better talk to our attorney, Justice Lapp."

Lucky rolled his eyes and ran out of Misericordia.

Jocko had hired Hervey Hamilton Lapp, the great legal philosopher who'd left the Supreme Court because he was sick of the other justices. He was seventy-nine years old. And Inertia's story intrigued him. The county prosecutors were scared to face Justice Lapp in open court. They couldn't defeat Kate Moss *and* the United States. They kept Katinka locked in the asylum. Justice Lapp subpoenaed the doctors' records and notes. The entire L.A. legal system began to quake. Lucky Brown met with Lapp.

"Herve," he said, "what about manslaughter? She sits a year or two in jail and . . ."

"She walks. My client will plead self-defense."

"That's ridiculous. She killed three men in cold blood."

"That's not how the jury will read it. Those men were kidnappers . . . and all of them had ravaged her."

Brown was young and ambitious, and he didn't want to tangle with an old fox, but he knew that any involvement with Lapp would bring him visibility. He might even get a movie offer. It was Hollywood. Anything could happen.

"Manslaughter, with a recommendation for leniency. Otherwise it's a duel."

"I can't wait."

The old fox lost his nerve the minute Lucky disappeared. It had nothing to do with the merits of the case. He could have crippled the whole county in his sleep. The gamin was innocent. He didn't care how many brutes she'd killed. Herve would weave a spell around the jury. He had a thick dossier on Katinka that his own clerks had assembled. He knew her past by heart, the horrors of a little Hurricane Lady. But he didn't trust his own past or present. Language itself had become a hurricane for Herve, a hurricane with black holes that could swallow him up in the middle of a sentence. He'd have a sudden lapse, and nothing, nothing could save him, not cue cards or clever assistants or notes on his sleeve . . .

He could have hailed a taxi, or summoned his chauffeur, but Herve wasn't an invalid. He drove himself to Misericordia. It took him half an hour to navigate twenty blocks. The boulevards seemed to escape him, the old landmarks had vanished. Nothing was familiar. He didn't panic. He found the hospital after a dozen false starts.

He went up to Robinson's room. The nurses and doctors recognized him, blushed in his presence. He was Hervey Hamilton Lapp, who'd fought his fellow justices and prepared dissenting opinions that were like slaps in the face.

Robinson was asleep. Herve sat by him until the young tycoon opened his eyes.

"Where am I?"

"At Misericordia . . . you were beaten by one of those brutes."

"Lucky Brown was here. He threatened me. Said . . ."

"It's his job to threaten. He's a public prosecutor. He prides himself on the cases he's won. I can assure you, Robinson, he has a very shallow reading of the law."

"Shouldn't we visit Katinka?"

"That's not a strategy I'd recommend. He has his spies at Echo Park. If we groom her, Lucky will know how to react. I'd rather leave her in virgin territory."

"But you haven't talked to her yet, haven't—"

"I have a much clearer picture this way. I can imagine what I need to imagine. And it will worry Brown. Robinson, I'd like to throw him off guard."

"Call me Jocko, please."

"But if I should falter . . . if I should lose my bearings in court, I'd like you to pinch my arm."

"Pinch your arm?"

"Exactly. I'd prefer to sit alone at the defense table. Without my legal team. The jury will love that . . . you'll be with me, Robinson. But you aren't a lawyer. And you have marks on your face. They'll score points for us. But it's important. The other thing."

"Pinching your arm."

Lucky Lucifer pounced. He had the court declare that Katinka was sane enough to stand trial. He moved her into the prison ward at the asylum. And suddenly Jocko was allowed to visit her. He got out of his bed at Misericordia and drove to Echo Park. The county had cut her hair. She wore a burlap dress that looked like a potato sack. Her face was green under the glaring lights. She was on the other side of a glass wall. He had to bark into a microphone.

"Tinka, wish I could stroke your hair."

"Stroke," she said. "Are you the Lamplighter? Where's Uncle Lionello?"

"In heaven," Jocko said.

She smiled. "I'm glad."

And she went back to her ward.

She'd lost her status as the princess of Echo Park. The nurses stopped being gentle. The guards didn't ask for her autograph. They'd driven her out of the main hospital ward like a wild animal and enclosed her in a cell without sunlight or a TV or a shelf for her books. She had to wear a rough gown that scratched her skin, and the guards wouldn't even lend her a shower curtain. They'd cluck at her while she was under the shower's icy needles, stare at her breasts.

"We can't save you, princess. You belong to Lucky Lucifer now."

They'd probe her body like fiendish gynecologists, subject her to strip searches whenever she had to leave her cell. And they'd talk about Lucky Lucifer in front of her, as if she didn't exist. Lucky would get them a detective's shield, bring them into "God's house," the LAPD. All they had to do was "punish" Katinka, wear her out, until she was docile and couldn't damage Lucky's case.

She began to hear the big bell and thought she was back in Cologne. She'd hurl her food tray at the guards, who had to force-feed her.

"Lucky doesn't want you to die. He can't get a conviction if you're a ghost."

A man came into her cell, whacked the guards

with his briefcase. He didn't have a cruel mouth, like the guards themselves. He sat with Katinka.

"Do you know who I am?"

"Lucky Lucifer."

"And what am I after?"

"My scalp."

Lucky laughed. "I'm gonna ask for mercy. But you can't cry in court. You have to sit on your chair like a church warden, pretend that you're sane. Promise? And you can't tell anyone that I was here. You have to disremember me."

38

Katinka arrived at county court with a busload of women in leg irons. She was wearing the same burlap dress. The bus ride had confused her. She saw Jocko behind a table, asked him what had happened to the Dom. She couldn't hear the big bell ring.

His eyes were black and blue. "The bell can't travel," he said.

She recognized the man she was supposed to forget. Lucky Lucifer. He called Miles Farmer to the stand. He'd have to tiptoe around the jury. The fools at the asylum hadn't bothered to change Katinka's clothes, and the jury kept staring at this princess in the burlap gown.

"Mr. Farmer, what's your relation to the accused?"

"I employ her sometimes . . . as a danseuse."

"Will you explain that?"

"She danced and modeled at different shows. It was a way of drawing men into a net. She'd gather certain information and then Mr. Carelli and Mr. Schill would rob them of their assets."

Miles painted Katinka as a criminal who had a falling out with her partners, Lionello, Waldie, and Lothar, and seized the moment to kill them, just as she'd killed her own dad.

Lucky seemed confident now; he turned Miles over to Justice Lapp. The old man would sink into oblivion. All Lucky had to do was wait. . . . But Herve sprang up from the defense table like some brilliant ballet master. There was no mist in his eyes. He shuffled through several cards, found the right one, and started to badger Miles. "Did you witness the assassination of Sergeant Baer?"

"I wasn't in Germany at the time."

"Has a corpse ever been found?"

"I don't think so."

"And he could be wandering the earth on one more of his crooked deals."

"It's possible."

The old fox turned his back on Miles Farmer and faced the jury. "Did you or did you not help plan the kidnapping of Jocko Robinson?"

"Waldie did all the planning. I only followed."

"And what was his motive?"

"Waldie didn't need a motive. He did what popped into his head."

"Just like that?"

"He was jealous of Jocko."

"And . . ."

"He wanted Jocko dead. But he wouldn't have killed him."

Herve tapped on the witness box with two fingers.

"Did he . . . did he intend . . ."

He was lost in his own little garden. He couldn't remember a single name. The storm had struck, uprooted all his grammar, left him in a hurricane of meaningless words and signs. He couldn't remember if he had a wife or children, where he was born, how old he was, what he was doing in this sea of faces. Was he supposed to dance? I'm Harvey Hambone, the minstrel from Miami. I . . .

He felt a tug, as if a baby alligator had bitten his elbow.

He cried out, "Help me, I'm Hamilton Lapp."

The judge seemed alarmed. He idolized the old fox, was in awe of him. "Are you all right, Mr. Justice? Should I call a recess? You can sit in my chambers and . . ."

"I'm fine," the old fox sang. Jocko Robinson stood behind him, and he whispered in Jocko's ear. "One pinch is enough. You can go back to the table."

And then he did start to dance as he looked into the jury's eyes and returned to his attack.

"Farmer, did Waldie Reynolds intend to let Mr. Robinson go?"

"Tomorrow," Miles said, "today . . . I don't know."

"But you do know."

"Objection," said Lucky Lucifer. "Counsel is leading my witness, toying with him."

"Overruled," said the judge. "But please get to the point, Mr. Justice."

"I will," said the old fox, bowing to judge and jury. He felt like the king of this court. He growled at Miles. His memory wouldn't fail him now.

"Did Mr. Reynolds ever talk of doing grievous bodily harm to Mr. Robinson?"

"He was always talking . . . and he was crazy about Tinka."

"When did he intend to let Mr. Robinson go?"

Miles blinked at Lucky Lucifer, shut his eyes, and whispered one word.

"The court can't hear you, Farmer."

"Never," Miles said. "Waldie was gonna keep him for life."

"And did the accused sense the gravity of the situation?"

"I think so."

"And if she was so murderous, so involved with shedding blood, why didn't she destroy you?"

"Me? I'm a show runner . . . I couldn't have hurt Katinka."

"Then would you call her a homicidal lady?"

"No. I'd call her a damaged child."

Lucky looked at the jurors, who were holding handkerchiefs to their eyes, looked at Katinka in her penitent's gown, looked at the old fox, and realized that he'd just lost the biggest case of his life.

Jocko rented a remote little cottage at the Chateau Marmont, where he could hide with Katinka away from the hurly-burly of Hollywood and still live next to Duck Soup. Her eyes would wander, as if she were dreaming of the Dom.

Sunshine showed up. He was adrift without Katinka.

"Karl, you have to stop catching for her. She isn't Kate Moss. She doesn't model anymore."

Karl hugged Katinka, and both of them started to cry.

"Wear a scarf summer and winter," Karl said, "or you'll catch tonsillitis."

"Karly, they took my tonsils out."

"It doesn't matter. You can still catch tonsillitis."

Jocko sent Sunshine back to Detroit with enough cash to open another shoe factory, and then he ran from Duck Soup with Katinka, returned to Washington Square . . .

Mr. Robinson didn't look at Jocko when he opened the door. He was staring at Katinka, and his face seemed to explode into a silly song. "Model for me . . . I'll give you the building."

And Inertia, who'd been silent on the plane, silent at the Chateau Marmont, silent at the insane asylum, also began to sing. "Uncle Rob, you'll make me blush. I'm practically engaged to your boy."

"But I need you more," the old man said. He calmed down, sniffled once, and decided to recognize Jocko. "Good to see you, son."

And Jocko moved into his monk's bedroom with Katinka.

It started to snow. There were little white mountains on every block. His dad sat in the living room and sobbed. Mr. Robinson had run out of bagels. "I'll starve to death . . . where's Katinka?"

She wasn't in bed when Jocko woke to a blinding wall of snow. She wasn't sitting in the tub, waiting for Jocko to wash her with a mitten.

"Did she disappear from your chicken coop, son? Is she modeling for other men? I told her. I was the better catch. You made too many demands on her. You didn't give the girl a rest."

"I'll strangle you, dad."

"Jack the Ripper. Get me some bagels. And don't forget Katinka. I can't digest a bagel without her green eyes."

Katinka wasn't lost in the snow. She hadn't even drifted away from Jocko. Skeleton had come to the door in the middle of the night, while Jocko and Uncle Rob were asleep.

"Tinka, we're in trouble . . . Alfonso's found us. He wants his cut. He says if you're married to the Lamplighter, you have to give up half."

"Half of what? I'm not married. I'm only engaged . . . and whose side are you on?"

"I'm neutral," Skeleton said. "But we have to eat."

"Are you strolling again?"

"With Alfonso. Who else do we have? You got rid of all our benefactors. We didn't starve when Lothar was around."

"And we didn't have a dime. Where's Alfonso?"

"At the Hide."

"He opened the club?"

"It isn't legal. He doesn't even have a liquor license. But it's the last home we have. He wants to see you. He insists."

"I don't like insisters."

"Tinka, he has the key to this apartment. Did you forget? He worked for Uncle Rob, gave him pedicures, massaged his feet."

"And stole money from his wallet . . . I was there."

"He's waiting for you, Tinka. He says he'll put another pig's tail on the Lamplighter's head."

"He'll suffer if he mutilates my man. Come on."

"But you aren't even dressed."

Inertia covered her nightgown with a coat, wrapped a scarf around her neck, found a pair of boots, and marched with Skeleton into the storm.

They had to navigate with their own bobbing heads, or they'd never have gotten to Wooster Street.

The Elephant's Hide was like a bat's cave. It didn't even have electricity. Alfonso lit his club with a whole forest of candles. Tinka laughed. She'd found the perfect decor to match her own savage will. Her shadow was gigantic on the wall.

There was no other heat than the candles' hissing wax. And the girls shivered with Alfonso, who was behind the bar, wearing a coat and scarf, like Katinka.

"I'm desperate," Alfonso said.

"What can I do?"

"You're an heiress now. You can hit the Lamplighter or the old man."

"And what if I refuse?"

"That's not an option. I'll scatter your lousy love nest. I'll break the old man's head. I'll—"

Katinka reached halfway across the bar to sock Alfonso, but Skeleton and Nightmare fell on top of her, and she had to claw at her own crew.

Alfonso started to groan. "I'm freezing. We can't pull in any customers. Who'll supply us with whiskey and champagne? We had to steal the candles. Nightmare seduced a clown on Canal Street. We're gonna die. We don't have enough to eat."

"You could take to the road."

"Without you? We wouldn't have a prayer. You were our Kate Moss."

"Shut up," Katinka said.

Alfonso came at her with a knife. She stood her

ground, her green eyes glowing in the pieces of candlelight. She slapped at Skeleton and Nightmare, slapped at the knife, pulled money out of her pockets and tossed it in Alfonso's face.

"You're a demon," he said. "Just like your dad."

She couldn't desert her band. Nightmare and Skeleton were like secret sisters. They sang to her while she lay upstairs at Der Papagei, fed her toast and black tea. She'd have to get the electricity turned back on, discover a magic pipeline to pink champagne.

"Children," she said, "I'll work two nights a week. But I'm not gonna do any Kate Moss numbers."

"You don't have to do any numbers," Nightmare said. "You'll still be Kate."

"Shut up. And none of you is going to bother the Lamplighter and Uncle Rob. Promise?"

"We promise," Skeleton said.

She turned to Alfonso. "Because if you make a dumb move, I'll disappear forever."

She hugged Nightmare and Skeleton, was about to leave. But something bothered her. She could hear a stirring in the Lamplighter's old office behind the bar, as if a gigantic rat were gnawing the walls. But it wasn't a rat. The door opened, and her dead father walked into the front room with a brace around his neck.

"Aren't you glad to see me, dear?"

The color flew out of her. She could have been a marionette in white paint. Skeleton and Nightmare had tricked her into coming here. That's what hurt the most.

"Tinka," Nightmare said, "your dad was gonna . . ."

"Quiet," the sergeant said. "No sad stories." He was clutching Carelli's dart, with the long green feather. "It's a nifty souvenir. Tinka, you know how hard it was to pull out of my neck? Ask Skeleton. It was like a major operation. Nightmare nursed me. We thought we'd all profit from my sudden death. But the King wasn't clever enough. He let Carelli run the show. And Carelli is tap dancing under the ground, thanks to you, my lovely. Don't I deserve a second chance? You'll deliver the Lamplighter to us . . . won't she, Karl?"

And her catcher came out of the office, with tears in his eyes. "Tinka, I couldn't go back to Detroit. I'm not a shoeman anymore."

"Then what are you, Karly?"

"A tough guy."

She couldn't laugh. She'd spoiled Karl, babied him. And he'd picked up all the bad habits of a mercenary.

"Daddy darling," she said, "it's just me and you. Because I'm not bringing the Lamplighter into this situation."

"Sunshine," Baer said, "help me tie her up."

"I can't. I can't harm Inertia."

The sergeant slapped him.

"Alfonso, grab her hands and feet."

But when Alfonso approached, she bit his face.

He howled. "Boss, she's a cannibal, worse than Carelli."

"What do I care?" the sergeant said. "I'm broke. Tinka, the government grabbed the King's accounts. You can't live on frozen assets. It's the Lamplighter. He's the only jewel we have."

"No, daddy, you have it wrong."

She snatched the green feather right out of her father's fist, cracked him on the skull with the dart's swollen shaft, tore the plastic cuff from around his neck.

"Somebody, somebody save me from this bitch."

Tinka cracked him on the skull again. "That's for Don Philippe."

"Who the hell is he?"

"The cattleman from San Antonio that you killed."

"Tinka, I never even touched him . . ."

She couldn't forget Philippe, how he'd carried her down the river in his gondola, knowing that she belonged to Lionello and Daddy Baer.

"Should we do the Russian polka? Should we celebrate?"

"Celebrate? I'm like a goddamn chicken who has to be fed through a hole in his neck. I'll have the hole for life. I need compensation and I need it quick."

"Who owns you, daddy dear?"

The sergeant didn't hesitate. He was an army man. He understood the chains of command. "Tinka owns me," he said. "But don't turn your back. I'll demolish you the first—"

She struck him harder, more deliberate. He landed in Skeleton's lap. "Where's my neck brace?"

"Remember," she said, "two nights a week. That's all the time I have to spare."

Karl followed her to the door.

"Tinka, can I go with you?"

"No, Karly. You picked your nest. Now live in it."

She scampered out of Alfonso's cave in her boots. It was delicious, almost. Suddenly she had her own gang. But she couldn't tell the Lamplighter about it. He wouldn't have understood her loyalty to such ambiguous girls. She was a soldier, like her dad. She had to protect her platoon, even if it meant lying to the Lamplighter a little. But she still had to bluff her way back to Washington Square in a blizzard.

Jocko ran downstairs in his boy's galoshes and his Banana Republic coat. All the bagel bins were empty. He trudged from store to store and finally ransomed the last bagel from a Greek coffee shop. He was forlorn without Katinka. Was it the banditry in her blood that pulled at him? Her deep isolation? Her indifference to men and material things?

He was returning home with his bagel when he saw the top of a snow mountain begin to move. He dug at the snow with his bare hands. He wasn't making much progress until the mountain collapsed and Inertia fell into his arms, with her gold-rimmed glasses.

"Darling, what took you so long?" she sang, inventing her own song. "I was playing in the snow, and suddenly there was an avalanche . . . why are you crying? I'm the one who was trapped."

How could he explain? This was Jocko's destiny. Finding and losing Katinka in the snow. He brought her upstairs with the bagel. Mr. Robinson did a little dance near the door. He had his bagel and Inertia's green eyes.